*Rich, Radiant Slaughter*

*By Orania Papazoglou*

**RICH, RADIANT SLAUGHTER**
**DEATH'S SAVAGE PASSION**
**WICKED, LOVING MURDER**
**SWEET, SAVAGE DEATH**

# Rich, Radiant Slaughter

ORANIA PAPAZOGLOU

A CRIME CLUB BOOK
**Doubleday**
NEW YORK   LONDON   TORONTO   SYDNEY   AUCKLAND

With the exception of Gail Larson,
all of the characters in this book are fictitious,
and any resemblance to actual persons, living or
dead, is purely coincidental.
The author would like to thank Ms. Larson
for agreeing to appear in this book.

A Crime Club Book
Published by Doubleday, a division of
Bantam Doubleday Dell Publishing Group, Inc.
666 Fifth Avenue, New York, New York 10103

**Doubleday** and the portrayal of a man
with a gun are trademarks of
Doubleday, a division of Bantam Doubleday Dell
Publishing Group, Inc.

Library of Congress Cataloging-in-Publication Data

Papazoglou, Orania, 1951–
Rich, radiant slaughter / Orania Papazoglou. — 1st ed.
p.   cm.
I. Title.
PS3566.A613R53 1988
813'.54—dc19          88-19193
CIP

ISBN 0-385-24612-9

*This book is for Matthew William DeAndrea, who helped.*

*Rich, Radiant Slaughter*

From the Baltimore *Sun,* Monday, December 14:

# BOOK PARTY TO
# BENEFIT HOMELESS

Baltimore this week will be host to one of the most unusual charity drives in American history, the National Book Drive for Family Shelter. Organized by Evelyn Nesbitt Kleig of the New York publishing firm of Austin, Stoddard and Trapp, the tour, which has already done service in nine U.S. cities, brings best-selling authors to their fans for literary gossip, autograph signings, a celebrity auction and charity book sales. The tour benefits the Ad Hoc Committe for Advocacy for the Homeless, a group dedicated to finding acceptable housing for this country's approximately 50,000 homeless families.

Among the famous authors coming to Baltimore will be: **Phoebe Damereaux,** popular historical novelist and creator of this year's spectacular hit, *Timeless Love;* Pulitzer Prize-winning literary figure **Christopher Brand;** romance celebrity **Amelia Samson;** Christian family advocate **Tempesta Stewart;** and true-crime-author-cum-detective **Patience Campbell McKenna.**

Gail Larson, owner of The Butler Did It mystery bookstore on North Charles Street, will host a champagne book party for the visiting authors from four to seven Tuesday afternoon. Times and locations for other events will be announced tomorrow.

Expenses for the tour have been underwritten by billionaire recluse Jonathon Hancock Lowry. All proceeds for all events will go directly to AHCAH.

Persons wishing further information, or wishing to volunteer their time to the enterprise, should contact Mrs. Margaret Johnson Keeley of the Baltimore Book Lovers Association at . . .

# ONE

It started on one of those days that could have been the opening of a John Carpenter movie, and because of that wasn't much good as the opening of anything else at all. Great banks of black clouds, distant thunder, intermittent attacks of sleet: the train shuddered and swayed through freeze-frame tableaux of twisted metal, using the weather for a metaphor. What the metaphor was supposed to mean, I didn't know. For one thing, I was tired. The twisted metal was the minor industrial district on the outskirts of Baltimore. Baltimore was the tenth stop in a ten-city, four-week charity book tour I'd been on since its beginning in New York. The last time I'd had a full night's sleep, I'd been back in Manhattan. The last time I'd sat down to a meal that wasn't fast food or rubber chicken, I'd been in New Orleans—and that had been almost ten days ago. I'd gotten to that point in the private history of exhaustion where the material world seems to be disintegrating.

My new reading glasses slid down my nose, ruining my focus on page 264 of *Whispers of Romance* for the third time in six minutes. I turned the book over in my lap and took the glasses off. In spite of its title, *Whispers of Romance* was not a novel. It was—at least theoretically—a work of nonfiction devoted to an exploration of "the romantic suspense novel as a paradigm and determinant of traditional female consciousness." It read like the kind of book that would have a line like that on its cover, and it was just as self-indulgent and confused as I'd expected it to be. Someday, somebody is going to write a book about romance novels and romance readers who actually knows something about one or the other. At that point, I'll be able to sit down with a book that calls itself "a study" and not be subjected to pseudo-feminist fantasies about brainwashed ninnies working themselves to the bone to forge their own chains. Until then, I had *Whispers of Romance,* a book deemed "feminist" because of its hatred of women by a woman so politicized she went into spasms of Marxian dialectics every time she stubbed her toe.

Across the narrow gap between our facing seats, Phoebe was reading Hazel Ganz's latest, *Passionate Time.* It looked a hell of a lot better than *Whispers of Romance,* but everything did. I stuck out my foot and kicked her lightly in the ankle. I could have hit her ankle if she'd been on the other side of the aisle and a full seat up. I am six feet tall and almost all legs. I have the kind of body the magazines want everybody to have—which drives the pseudo-feminists even crazier than romance novels do.

Phoebe does not have the kind of body women are supposed to have —or ever have been supposed to have, in the entire history of civilization. She is four foot eleven. She weighs a hundred thirty pounds. Dressed up for a public appearance, in full Phoebe Damereaux regalia, she looks like an overdecorated dwarf Christmas tree in perpetual motion. She was dressed in full Phoebe Damereaux regalia that morning, even though it was barely seven o'clock and we were on a train. Floor-length jade-green velvet caftan, nine strands of twenty-four-inch rope diamonds, diamond globe earrings big enough to use as crystal balls, ostrich-feather hair combs in her wiry black hair: at the terminal in Baltimore there would be press, and Phoebe would be ready for them. She had a reputation to maintain.

She also had what looked like an incipient weight problem. The caftan was tight. I paid as much attention to that as I could—I really was tired—and then decided I was imagining things. In her way, Phoebe had always had a "weight problem." She'd always been heavier than the insurance charts said she ought to be. In another way, she'd never had a "problem" at all. Her weight had been stable for as long as I'd known her, all the way back to our freshman year at Greyson College for Women. Being, like many very thin people, a near neurotic about weight, I knew that people who have weighed one thing for many years don't tend to gain or lose with any speed, unless they're ill. Phoebe certainly didn't look ill. In fact, she looked better than she ever had.

She stuck the torn-off end of a pack of Mamma Leone matches into *Passionate Time* and put it on the seat beside her. There were dozens of other people on this tour, including the entire executive board of the American Writers of Romance, but we were the only ones up and moving early enough to make it to breakfast in the dining car. Even Evelyn Nesbitt Kleig, the publicist for Austin, Stoddard and Trapp who had organized this mess, had remained safely barricaded in her Pullman sleeper.

"How is that?" Phoebe said, gesturing to the book on my lap.

I shrugged. "How am I supposed to know?"

"I take it that means it's dismal."

"The phenomenological-existential interface of expectation and reality tends to cause both psychological and emotional dissonance in the spatiotemporal arena."

"Oh dear."

"It might not be so bad if I knew what it meant."

"Does the writer know what it means?" Phoebe said.

"No."

"Well. You don't actually have to read the whole thing through, you know. You're only trying to decide what to vote for for the award. You must know by now you're not going to vote for that thing."

"Don't you read them all the way through?"

"Well, yes. But these are novels."

"Bad novels," I pointed out. "Some of them, anyway."

"Fortunately, Hazel's isn't one of the bad ones," Phoebe said. "I was getting a little nervous. Category is in such a mess. Nobody's making any money. Second Chance at Love went down to two books a month. For a while there, it looked like they were going to stop publishing altogether. Advances are down to twenty-five hundred dollars a book. It's really much better for Hazel to be doing historicals. I was beginning to wonder how she was going to keep her son at Groton."

"Hazel has a son at Groton?" Hazel was not only the archetypical Midwestern housewife, she *looked* like the archetypical Midwestern housewife. Calico shirtwaist dresses. One-inch stack-heeled shoes. "Good" cloth coats in sensible navy blues and at-least-it-won't-show-the-dirt dark grays. The idea of her showing up at a Groton Parents' Day, with all those people in natural ranch mink and customized Rolls-Royce limousines, was staggering.

I took *Whispers of Romance* off my lap and pitched it onto the seat beside *Passionate Time,* not bothering to mark my place. "Maybe the AWR should consider giving up the nonfiction award," I said. "Half the time you can't think of anybody to give it to. The people who write these things just want a chance to prove how intellectual they are. And avant-garde. And politically correct. Then people like me have to read the damn things, and I don't even *belong* to the AWR."

"Are you sorry you agreed to do it?" Phoebe said. "I mean, I know how you feel about the convention, and I wouldn't have asked except—"

"Except *nobody* wants to read these things."

Phoebe blushed. "Amelia threatened to firebomb us or something if I made her sit on the nonfiction committee again. And Hazel—"

"I'm sure they all had good excuses, Phoebe."

"But you *write* nonfiction," Phoebe said. "And you've *won* the award—"

"I won it because it was one of those years you had nobody else to give it to."

"Whatever. You like romance writers. You like romance novels. You get published in *The Atlantic*. You're very respectable, Patience. And besides—"

"And besides," I said, "you knew damn well you could talk me into it, because you know damn well you can talk me into anything."

Phoebe looked away. "I wonder where Evelyn is," she said. "We're practically there."

I got my cigarettes out of the pocket of my jeans—Phoebe knows never to put me anywhere but in smoking sections—and put the whole matter of the Charlotte Brontë Award for Best Nonfiction Book About Romance out of my head. Back in the days when I'd been writing romance, I'd taken it all very seriously. Now I wrote true crime. I kept up with romance because Phoebe and I were close, and with the American Writers of Romance because I'd known most of them forever and liked them all. Almost all. I thought about Miss Tempesta Stewart, Grand High Pooh-Bah of born-again Christian romance, back there somewhere in one of the sleeping compartments. I put *her* out of my head, too. She was an unpleasant reminder of the fact that, since the world did not stand still, the world of romance writers and romance readers and romance novels wouldn't stand still either. In the good old days it had been all optimism and high ideals and sisterly solidarity on a scale Manhattan Radical Feminists couldn't manage if they started cloning themselves. Now . . . I shook my head. The Good Old Days. 1984. I wasn't just exhausted, I was losing it. And did I really think the years I'd spent in a third-floor walk-up closet on West Eighty-second Street were *better* than the ones I'd spent in a twelve-room prewar co-op on Central Park West?

Maybe I did. Sometimes. When I wasn't thinking straight.

My mother always says I have less common sense than a gnat.

Phoebe started up from the opposite seat, blanched, grabbed the unsteady seat arm to steady herself. I looked up, surprised and a little concerned. Phoebe had literally turned green. I'd always thought that was only a figure of speech.

"Are you all right?" I said. "You look—"

"Tuna fish." Phoebe smiled weakly. "It must have been the tuna fish."

"What must have been the tuna fish?"

"At that place in Jackson, or wherever it was we stopped last night. I bought a tuna fish sandwich at a stand. Don't you remember?"

"No."

"Well, I did. And ever since I've been feeling a little—"

"Sick," I said.

"Exactly," she said.

"We ought to get you to a doctor."

Phoebe shook her head violently. "No, no," she said. "I'm really fine. I just feel a little—sort of seasick, that's all. It'll go away in a couple of hours. I think I'll just go down to the ladies' room here—"

"Do you want some help?"

"Of course I don't want some help. I'm just going to the ladies' room. Finish *Whispers of Romance.* Then you can spend the time in Baltimore running up phone bills to Nick and Adrienne and reading Hazel's book."

She lurched into the aisle, staggering against the motion of the train. I bit my lip. She really did look sick—as sick as I'd felt one year and three months before, when I'd swallowed a Styrofoam cup of arsenic-laced coffee and nearly died. I knew she was lying to me, too. She hadn't had a tuna fish sandwich, in Jackson or anywhere else, the night before. What she had had was one half of a gigantic pecan cinnamon bun. I knew that because I was the person who had had the other half.

I watched her disappear through the safety door at the end of the aisle and turned my head to go back to staring out the window. The weather seemed to be getting worse. The black clouds no longer looked like clouds at all, but like great flat sheets of fire-damaged metal, a celestial manhole cover shutting us away from the sky. The red and green and gold of the Christmas ornaments that had been hung along the signal posts every few feet of track looked dispirited and limp. The sleet was rapidly turning into hail. *It was a dark and stormy night,* I thought, and then I amended it. It wasn't night at all. According to the digital clock on the side of the terminal coming up ahead of us, it was 7:15 in the morning.

Sick in Baltimore. Sick in Jackson. Sick in New Orleans. Sick in Sherman Oaks, too—although Phoebe thought I didn't know about that. I'd taken off to the lobby just before she'd taken off to the bathroom. Halfway to the elevators, I'd realized I'd forgotten my wallet. When I'd let myself back into our hotel room, I'd heard her through the wall—heaving like someone who has just taken an overdose of ipecac.

My cigarette had burned into a long column of ash. I tapped it into the inadequate metal ashtray on the arm of my seat and started to gather up my things. The train was slowing to a stop.

It wasn't the *fact* that Phoebe was pregnant that bothered me. That can happen to anyone, especially someone like Phoebe, whose sexual experience had been limited to David Grossman, my fiancé's law partner and the man she had been seeing for the past three years. I wasn't worried about the out-of-wedlock part either. Nick and I were the ones who had a wedding on the calendar—eight weeks away—but Phoebe and David had been heading in that direction for months. It was going to happen sooner or later. A baby would just make it happen sooner. My private opinion was that Phoebe would make a great mother. She had changed her name from Weiss to Damereaux when she started writing the books that would turn her into the biggest thing to hit historical romance since the death of Georgette Heyer, but she had never really abandoned the Weiss part. She was the kind of woman whose children would never be satisfied with anybody else's cooking, including their own. And for good reason.

There was a hiss and a squeal and a shriek, and we came to a stop. Outside, on the wall over the door to the waiting room, I could just see a hand-lettered cloth banner that said: WELCOME BOOK TOUR. BALTI-

MORE WELCOMES THE NATIONAL BOOK DRIVE FOR FAMILY SHELTER. DECEMBER 15–18.

I got Phoebe's overnight bag from the shelf above my head and set it down in the aisle. No, it wasn't the *fact* that Phoebe was pregnant that was bothering me. It was the fact that she hadn't told me one damn thing about it.

Phoebe and I had been as close as Siamese twins for eighteen years. We'd been through poverty together. We'd been through the various stages and uncertainties of success, although Phoebe was more successful than I could ever be. Phoebe had introduced me to Nick. Nick and I had introduced her to David. When I'd wanted to adopt the eight-year-old daughter of a murdered woman I had known briefly before her death, Phoebe had gone to war with the New York State Department of Public Welfare to make sure the adoption went through. When Phoebe had been rejected for an apartment by a co-op board composed of people who still thought of anti-Semitism as fashionable, I'd used my family connections to change their minds. There are people who say that women—especially women who stubbornly refuse to have their consciousnesses raised—can never really be friends. I knew it wasn't true.

Which meant, as far as I was concerned, that the situation as it stood that day in Baltimore made absolutely no sense at all.

# TWO

When I'd first heard about the National Book Drive for Family Shelter, I'd thought of it as just another rip-off of Bob Geldof and Band Aid. As an analysis, that made a certain amount of sense. The setup was right. A whole collection of authors, popular and prestigious, would get on a train and go from one city to the next across the United States, giving interviews, signing autographs and—most important—selling books. The money from the book sales would be donated to an organization called the Ad Hoc Committee for Advocacy for the Homeless. The Ad Hoc Committee—they liked to call themselves The Housing Project—would use the money to find shelter for families with small children and no place to live. As a charity, it had it all over the publishing community's last foray into good works, meaning the literacy drive. The literacy drive had turned out to have a few kinks in it, at least for the sort of people who like to describe themselves as "thoughtful" and "compassionate," which almost everybody connected to books does. One of the things "thoughtful" and "compassionate" people abhor is lending their names to anything that might be construed, even if only by an act of aggressive irrationality, "racist, sexist or ethnocentric." With the literacy drive, practically anything anybody did fell into one of those categories, and quite a few things fell into all three. Holding Shakespeare Appreciation Seminars was declared to be "perpetuating patriarchal stereotypes of women." Passing out free copies of *The Wizard of Oz* was denounced as "promoting anti-aspirational negativism." Even the health-food nuts got into the act. *They* didn't like *Catcher in the Rye,* although their reasons were slightly different from the ones put forward by conservative school boards. Conservative school boards didn't like *Catcher* because it had the f-word in it. Health-food nuts didn't like it because the hero ate junk food, and the example of a hero eating junk food might, well, incite children to ruin their teeth. Homelessness was a much better cause.

Even conservatives couldn't hate a project dedicated to solving a problem with private, rather than government, money. Even outright Marxists had to agree (at least in public) that it was better for everyone if the children had a warm bed to sleep in at night while the revolution was waiting to happen.

The analysis also made sense because of the person who was running the project: Evelyn Nesbitt Kleig, a junior publicist at Austin, Stoddard and Trapp, and a one-woman walking encyclopedia of fads, fashions, fanaticisms and foo-politics. I'd known Evelyn for three or four years—she'd been publicist on my first true-crime book (the one about the Agenworth murder, which won the Charlotte Brontë Award), and again on my most recent, *Blood Red Romance*—and on one level I didn't understand her at all. She was a young woman, no more than twenty-eight or twenty-nine. She talked like one. She dressed like one. She just didn't act like one. Where most of her contemporaries spent their weekends at singles bars or networking parties, Evelyn spent hers working for charities. I come from one of those very old New England families where volunteer service is a kind of sacrament. My mother is the mainstay of the Connecticut branches of everything from the American Cancer Society to the Friends of the Metropolitan Opera. Even with all that in my background, I found Evelyn stupefying. It wasn't so much the charities she chose—although there *had* been something called the Gay and Lesbian Vegetarian Action Army Task Force for the Struggle for Social Justice in a New Age—as the sheer number of them. "Educational efforts" to alert the public to the dangers inherent in allowing municipal governments to erect nativity scenes in public parks, fund drives to provide free condoms to the habitués of shooting galleries, organizations formed to Bring the Truth about Nuclear War to the inmates of daycare centers—if it needed money and promised to be totally ineffectual, Evelyn was right in the middle of it. She even crossed the great divide between political obsessions. She worked as hard for the Center For Educational Choice—which was a group advocating the teaching of Genesis in high school biology classes—as she did for the Institute for Secular Ecology. The Institute for Secular Ecology was trying to get all mention of God removed from the Declaration of Independence.

What Evelyn didn't do was have boyfriends, go on dates or waste her time at merely social gatherings. In all the years I had known her, I had never once heard her mention a single person, male or female, unconnected to her by paid or volunteer work. As far as I could tell, Evelyn Nesbitt Kleig didn't have a private life. She might not even know what one was.

There was something else she didn't do, and that was where my original analysis of the National Book Drive as a Bob Geldof rip-off fell down. Most of the imitators who have taken the Band Aid concept and run with it have been interested as much in their own personal glory as in any good they might do. Evelyn was definitely not interested in that. She had a thousand chances to promote herself. The reporters who had come to greet us in every city we visited would have been more than happy to have a story on the woman behind the scenes. Evelyn wasn't having any. She herded us around like a sheep dog at shearing season. She made sure we got to the right places at the right times. She melted into the woodwork. After four weeks and nine cities, I was almost ready to admit her motives were entirely pure.

Almost, but not quite.

I stood at the door to the waiting room, under the hand-lettered cloth banner, and stared into the cavernous space inside while giving Phoebe a chance to catch up. A long table covered with a series of thin white cloths had been set up in the middle of the wooden benches, with microphones strewn across the top and gray metal folding chairs shoved into a row at the back. In front of this table were the assembled representatives of the Baltimore local media, plus a camera crew from CBS News. In back of it, Christopher Brand and Tempesta Stewart were fighting for the right to the center space. Evelyn was off to the side, her Cyndi Lauper-look-alike outfit hidden under a heavy winter coat. With her was our benefactor and chief underwriter, Jonathon Hancock Lowry, the one the press always called a "billionaire recluse." That wasn't entirely accurate. He wasn't really a billionaire— the fortune he'd inherited had topped out at eight hundred fifty million. He wasn't really a recluse either. He was just a twenty-two-year-old boy with too little meat on his bones and too much Adam's apple —who'd been kept as sealed off from the real world as any fragile fledgling of an endangered species, until the day he turned eighteen and was handed both his freedom and the country's largest hereditary fortune in a single stroke. Jon Lowry was almost terminally shy. He'd been taught by tutors at home instead of being sent to school. He'd been forbidden the company of other children for fear he'd catch "germs." He'd been as completely cut off from the world as his crazy Aunt Gertrude had been able to get him, which was very cut off indeed. When he'd expressed an interest in going to Disneyland, she'd had a complete mini-amusement park—Ferris wheel, roller coaster, and carousel—built on the grounds of the two-hundred-acre Lowry estate.

Now Jon Lowry was out in the world, and he literally didn't know what to do there. He'd wandered into an open meeting for the Housing Project, attached himself to Evelyn and refused to let go. Either Evelyn had convinced him of the very same thing she'd convinced herself—meaning that the stars of the tour were the authors, and nobody else should interfere—or she'd *failed* to convince him to perform for the cameras for the sake of charity. Neither proposition made much sense. Best-selling authors like Phoebe and Tempesta and Christopher Brand would bring in a lot of people to buy books, but the appearance of a famous "billionaire recluse" would bring in even more. Hell, he'd bring in people who had never bought a book. And although he was shy, he was more than merely "attached" to Evelyn. I'd had the distinct impression throughout the tour that if Evelyn had asked him to carry her piggyback from New Orleans to Minneapolis, he'd have done it.

I heard footsteps behind me and turned around. Phoebe was staggering to the waiting-room door, looking almost as green as she had when I'd left her back at the train. I turned away—if she wasn't going to tell me, I wasn't going to ask her—and gestured at the scene inside.

"Look at that," I said, meaning Tempesta and Christopher. "The Guru of Sexual Indulgence and the High Priestess of Premarital Virginity. Who do you think will win?"

"Amelia," Phoebe said.

"Amelia isn't there."

"Look."

I looked. There was a churning in the crowd at the back. A moment later, Amelia Samson, the eighty-two-year-old Queen of American category romance, pushed her way through to the table. A split second after that, she was firmly and irretrievably ensconced in the center chair. The mainstream press likes to paint romance writers as pink, fluffy little things, with dithering brains and vague smiles and a passionate desire to please. Amelia Samson was five-ten and weighed two-forty. She had spent her twenties running a mangle in a steam laundry, in the days before all that was automated. The muscular development of her shoulders and upper arms was awesome. She looked like a linebacker—or would have, if she hadn't been wearing a beaded Worth traveling suit just as well-armored and well-constructed as she was herself. Christopher Brand worked out with weights two hours a day seven days a week. Amelia could have crumpled him up like a piece of paper.

"And at her age, too," I said. "Good old Amelia."

"Look at Hazel," Phoebe said. "She looks ready to bust a gut."

Hazel did indeed look ready to bust a gut. She was a traditional romance writer, as "traditional" had been defined since the Great Romance Boom of 1980. She didn't like Christopher Brand because he was a "literary" writer, one of the breed who always seemed to be working overtime to make people like Hazel and the work they did seem totally worthless. She didn't like Tempesta Stewart because Tempesta—as Hazel had put it at the meeting that had elected Tempesta to the executive board of the AWR in spite of Hazel's efforts—represented a "step backward." Did we really want to go back to the days when romance novels ended at the closing of the bedroom door? Of course we didn't.

Phoebe tugged at the sleeve of my sweater. "Who's that?" she said. "Over there on the left. They're not press. They look official."

I followed the direction of her pointing finger. "Oh," I said. "The blonde is Gail Larson. She owns The Butler Did It."

"The Butler Did It?"

"The Butler Did It is the store we're supposed to sign at tonight. Are you sure you're all right? You never forget—"

"Who's the other one?"

The other one was a woman on the far end of her fifties, with one of those smooth gray helmets of hair that always look as though they might really be hats. She had on a blue gabardine suit and a little pinched pout—as if she did a lot of things she thought she wasn't properly appreciated for. I made a face. I'd never seen her before, but I could guess who she was. There had been someone like her in every city on the tour. For some reason, all enterprises concerned with books attract a fair percentage of the sort of people who get their kicks making sure nobody has any fun. They bludgeon their way into positions of power in the fan organizations. They attend open book parties in droves. They make life hell for everybody within screaming distance —and you have to be nice to them. The pleasant people are all so used to the inexpungible presence of these idiots, they've practically stopped volunteering to do any of the work that needs volunteers to get done.

I couldn't remember the name, so I rummaged around in my pockets until I found the crumpled sheet of paper with my Baltimore schedule on it. The only possibility leaped at me without my having to do any work at all.

"Try Mrs. Harold P. Keeley," I said.

"Mrs. Harold P. Keeley? Do people do that anymore? I mean, call themselves Mrs. John instead of Mary Smith."

"Some people do," I said. "Anyway, she's the only person on the list I wouldn't recognize. She's supposed to be the head of the Baltimore Book Lovers Association."

"Oh dear," Phoebe said.

"Do you ever wonder why things work out this way?" I said. "You can't do anything anymore without having it taken over by a lot of self-righteous fanatics. Self-righteous fanatics of the Left. Self-righteous fanatics of the Right. Self-righteous fanatics with no excuse at all except that they like being self-righteous fanatics. It's driving me crazy."

"Here comes Evelyn," Phoebe said. "She looks frantic. Do you ever wonder about *that?* Evelyn *always* looks frantic."

I did a one-hundred-eighty-degree turn and saw Evelyn bearing down on us, as frantic as Phoebe had said she was. When Evelyn got frantic—and Phoebe was right, it happened often—even her hair seemed to be electrified.

She skidded to a stop in front of us, her coat flapping open to reveal a Day-Glo orange miniskirt constructed in tiers.

"Patience!" she said. "Phoebe! You can't stand here all day. We have to get started."

"I don't think they need us to get started," I said. "Amelia's giving them a lecture."

Evelyn's head twisted around on her neck, far enough and fast enough to make me think (inevitably) of the little girl in *The Exorcist.* Then it started to swivel back, and stopped in mid-slide. She stared at Gail Larson and the woman I thought must be Mrs. Harold P. Keeley and frowned.

"Damn," she said.

"Excuse me?" I said.

"What?" she said. She faced us again, biting her lip. "Sorry. There's just so much to do. Writers simply do not realize—"

"—how hard it is to run a book tour. I know all that, Evelyn. Phoebe and I—"

"Oh, Phoebe and you are all right. You're not crazy, at least. Unlike *some* people I could mention."

"Like Tempesta Stewart?" Phoebe asked, hopeful. Phoebe had made her reputation on the hottest sex scenes in the business. She didn't like Tempesta any more than Hazel did.

But Evelyn waved Tempesta away. "She's all right," she said, "as long as you don't let her do anything drastic. There was an incident in Nashville once with an abortion clinic. The one who drives *me* crazy is Christopher Brand. The arrogant little son of a bitch." She turned her head again, but not quite in the right direction. She was talking about Christopher Brand. She seemed to be looking at Jon Lowry. I wondered idly if there was something wrong with her eyes, or something on her mind we ought to know about.

She swiveled around again—it was like watching one of those jelly-roll toys you can buy in Appalachian Crafts Shops—and said, "You know why we've spent half this tour in mystery bookstores? Because of Christopher Brand, that's why. Practically nobody else would have him. They *have* had him. He's got the worst reputation in the history of book tours."

"He hasn't been bad on this one," I said. "I've hardly seen him."

"He hides in his closet and drinks," Evelyn snorted. "And then— well, never mind. Everything's worked out so far and we don't have that much to do in Baltimore. But even the chain stores won't have him, and he's such a big name he sells five hundred books anyplace he appears. He's just too much damn trouble. *And* they think he's danger-ous. *And* they're right."

"Dangerous how?" Phoebe perked up a little.

"He stabbed a bookstore clerk in Tacoma. It was only with a penknife, but still. Are you two going to come over and sit down? There goes the poster now."

The poster was a traveling announcement of who and what we were. The what came first, with a row of pictures underneath it. Under mine it said: PATIENCE CAMPBELL MCKENNA, NEW YORK TIMES BEST-SELLING AUTHOR OF BLOOD RED ROMANCE.

*Blood Red Romance* had made the *Times* list for exactly a week. So had my book on the Agenworth murder. The book that came between those two—an exposition of the deaths of several members of the Brookfield publishing family—had sunk out of sight without a trace.

I hooked the straps of my tote bag over my shoulder and took Phoebe by the arm.

"Into the fray once again," I said.

Phoebe shook her head. "No, no," she said. "I'm afraid I've got to—"

She shook my hand off and disappeared into the gathering crowd, her face as green as the velvet of her caftan.

I stuck a cigarette in my mouth and promised myself—*swore* to myself—that when this tour was over, I was going to sit that woman down and give her a talking to. I was going to give it to her in exactly the tone of voice my mother would have, and I wasn't going to shut up until she started making sense.

In the meantime, I had Christopher Brand, Tempesta Stewart, Amelia Samson, and CBS News. It was really too bad Evelyn didn't want to make personal capital out of this. The spadework she'd done must have been first-class.

I gave brief and not very serious thought to following Phoebe—just in case she *had* been poisoned—and headed for the press table.

# THREE

It was one of those situations that start out crazy and go positively lunatic in no time at all—and if I'd seen it coming, I'd have done what I *should* have done, right from the beginning. What I should have done was demand an explanation, if not then and there (CBS had been joined by ABC), then at least as soon as we got back to the hotel. Instead, I let myself be carried—first through the press conference ("Could you tell me, Miss McKenna, how it feels to make your living off of other people's pain?"); then through the cab ride out to the harbor ("If somebody doesn't do something about that little snot, I'm going to stick a pin in him"—Hazel Ganz on Christopher Brand); then up to the reception desk at the Sheraton Inner Harbor. By the time we got to the reception desk, all I could think of was that the Sheraton Inner Harbor, unlike most of the other hotels we'd stayed in for the tour, actually looked nice. It had a high-ceilinged, open-plan lobby with pretty carpets and furniture more domestic than industrial. It had a little Christmas tree in a planter, decorated with red and silver bulbs and tiny twinkling white lights. I'd heard rumors it had some of the best room service on earth.

The woman at the reception desk handed me a little white card and a ballpoint pen. I handed her my American Express card. Behind me, Christopher Brand lit up his pipe and silenced the chorus of staff objections before they started. There are a few advantages to having a reputation for physical violence.

He tapped me on the shoulder and said, "I don't get you. You don't want to screw, and I'm beginning to think you actually *like* those people."

"I don't want to screw you," I said. The Sheraton Inner Harbor might have some of the world's best room service, but like every other hotel in the world, it had a registration card that defied analysis by anyone who was self-employed, independently wealthy, or just plain out of work. I struggled with questions about work addresses and home phone numbers with my right hand and held up my left for Christopher's inspection. It was something I'd done two or three times in every city we'd visited, as if if I did it often enough, Christopher Brand would get the point. Nick is the epitome of a self-made man, which means that although he's doing very well, he doesn't like to spend money. He'd made an exception for my engagement ring, possibly because his mother (who thinks I'm wonderful) insisted on it. I had a mammoth pear-shaped diamond surrounded by tiny little sapphires. The quality was so good, that ring could have lit up a room with no electrical help.

It could not, however, get Christopher Brand's attention. He turned his back to the reception desk and looked down the line at our company. "You *do* actually like these people," he said. "You're an intelligent woman. Can't you tell they're idiots?"

"Idiots how?"

"Idiots," Christopher Brand said. "They've got IQs the size of golf scores."

I finished the registration card, put the pen down and pushed the whole mess toward the clerk. I decided not to say anything about the fact that a man with a Pulitzer should be able to come up with something better than the old insult about golf scores. Instead, I said, "You going to do that new tax thing they're making us do, with the expenses?"

"What? Of course I'm going to do it. I have to do it. Everybody has to do it. Christ, that's all I'd need. Ending up in tax court."

"Do you understand it?"

"Patience," he said, "nobody understands it. Even my accountant has a hard time understanding it. It doesn't make sense."

"It may not make sense, but *they* understand it." I nodded to the little clutch of people that included Phoebe, Hazel and Amelia. "They don't like it, but they do understand it. And they can explain it in plain English. And they can give you the court cases that make them think we'll eventually get rid of it."

"Patience, what's all this supposed to mean?"

"Oh," I said, "I don't know. I guess it's just that *I* feel like an idiot when I don't understand things, and *I* have a hard time calling people idiots when they can understand things I can't, so—"

"You're a bitch," Christopher Brand said. "Do you know that?"

"I don't just know it, I work at it."

"Yeah, well. If you don't—" He stopped. His face got that sucking-lemons look he'd become famous for, the one that made his eyes screw up into little pellets, like a pig's eyes. He made a gesture in the air that I recognized only because I'd spent some time playing poker with a few of Nick's less than well-mannered old friends from Queens, and said, "Jesus Christ. What's *she* doing here?"

I looked over his shoulder and caught her: Mrs. Harold P. Keeley, a felt-and-net hat over her indestructible hair, marching up the line importantly with a clipboard in her hand. I think I managed a sucking-lemons look of my own.

"I take it you're not going to defend *her,*" Christopher said. "God, I hate women like that."

"I'll admit she isn't the type to bring sweetness and light," I said.

"If you go all feminist on me, I'll kill you," he said. "There's always one of them, you ever notice that? Always. Cold-boxed little—"

"Do you really *have* to talk like an anatomy book written by a motor-cycle gang? All the time?"

"Can it. Women like that have ruined my life. If it hadn't been for—"

"If it hadn't been for what?"

"Never mind. I keep forgetting you're consorting with the enemy."

Romance writers are some of the best-natured people on earth, nothing at all like the Mrs. Harold P. Keeleys. Given the deluge of rot they have to put up with, they have to be. I thought about telling Christopher Brand all that, and decided not to. It wasn't what he wanted to hear, and he'd gone to work on his registration form anyway. I took back my American Express card, tucked it into the zippered compartment on the inside of my tote bag—like many New Yorkers, I never carry credit cards in anything that can be easily lifted or hidden in a pair of jeans—and drifted away.

I was halfway down the line when Mrs. Harold P. Keeley caught up with me, clipboard and all. Behind her was someone I hadn't noticed before, probably because she was slinking: Gail Larson. I gave Gail a little smile, letting her know I remembered we'd met before, and turned my attention to Mrs. Harold. I thought I might as well get it over with. At the end of the line, the romance writers were looking murderous.

"McKenna," Mrs. Harold P. Keeley said, checking something off on her board. "Patience Campbell McKenna."

"That's right," I said. "Do you always call yourself Mrs. Harold P.?"

"Excuse me?"

"Mrs. Harold P.," I said again. "Instead of your given name. I mean—"

"I haven't asked you to call me by my given name," she said.

"Margaret," Gail Larson said, sounding more than a little desperate. "Her name is Margaret."

"I'm twenty years older than you," Margaret Keeley said, "and I haven't *asked* you to call me Margaret."

"You asked *me* to call you Margaret," Gail Larson said. "Pay's been a very good friend to the store. So if you'll please—"

"It's what happens to people when they live in New York," Margaret Keeley said. "They get the wrong idea about books."

"I'm sorry," I said. "I don't understand—"

"Never mind," Gail Larson said. "Nobody understands."

"You *ought* to understand," Margaret Keeley said. "You ought to be more like *that* woman." She pointed across the lobby at Tempesta Stewart, struggling with a Mount Everest of Gucci bags a few feet away from the Christmas tree. "Miss Stewart is my very favorite writer. You don't know how *thrilled* I am to be able to meet her. If she hadn't been part of this, I'd never have gotten involved in it myself."

Gail sent her eyes ceilingward. I choked back a cough. Since there was an ashtray at my elbow, I got out my cigarettes and lit up. Margaret Keeley seemed about to deliver a lecture on the evils of smoking, and then to change her mind. She looked down at her clipboard again and frowned.

"You write true crime?"

"I write about historically true murders, yes," I said.

"Ordinary murders, or the—the sordid kind?"

"I suppose all murders are sordid," I said. "I'm not sure I know what you're getting at, Mrs. Keeley."

"Sex," Gail Larson said. "She's getting at sex."

"Oh," I said.

"I'm not *getting at* sex," Margaret Keeley said. "I'm simply trying to determine who will and who will not be suitable for the Cardington School. I teach at the Cardington School."

"What's the Cardington School?" I said.

"I've told her and told her," Gail Larson said. "Margaret, these people just don't have the time to give a speech at—"

"Miss Stewart has the time," Margaret Keeley said. "She told me so herself. As for the rest of these people—" She looked me up and down, making me feel like a Maypole inexplicably decked out in off-the-rack Gloria Sachs. "The Cardington School is a character-forming institution. We try to *mold* our students into moral, industrious, upstanding citizens of the community. We are trying to combat—not that it always works, of course."

"No," I said, "I don't suppose it does."

"Some people," Margaret Keeley said. Then she faltered a little, as if she'd just been reminded of something that blew all her assumptions out of the water. She looked down at her clipboard and tapped it once or twice with her pen. The pen was one of those silver-plate models that come in gift boxes with matching silver-plate pencils. Margaret Keeley rolled it between her fingers and scratched at its surface with a single blunt, clear-polished nail.

"Well," she said. "I don't suppose it matters. I don't think you'll do at all."

"For the Cardington School?" I said.

"Exactly," she said. She turned to look at Christopher Brand, still working at his registration form. He seemed to be having some kind of argument with the clerk, but it was hard to tell. Christopher Brand always seemed to be having arguments with everybody.

"I don't suppose he'll do either," she said, "but I might as well go talk to him. If I didn't talk to him, it would look funny, wouldn't it? Him with a Pulitzer Prize and everything. In *my* day, they didn't give prizes to people who used that kind of language. They didn't print that kind of language."

She tucked her clipboard under her arm and went marching off, a dumpy little pouter pigeon with heavy legs.

Gail Larson let out a great gust of air, making her fine blond fringe ripple. Normally, she is one of the most energetic women on earth, the kind of person who seems to be able to move without stopping, or even slowing down, for days at a time. Now she seemed deflated and depressed—and exasperated to the point of eruption.

"Oh God," she said. "That *woman.*"

"Who is she exactly, anyway?"

"Oh," Gail said, "that's hard to tell. I mean, she's got this husband, but you practically never see him. And she's got the Baltimore Book Lovers Association, but she's had that for years, and nobody ever paid attention to it until Evelyn heard about it. And it's all my fault. Evelyn heard about it through me."

"Why through you?"

"Margaret," Gail said, "is The Butler Did It's best customer."

"Margaret Keeley buys mystery books?"

"Six or seven hundred dollars' worth of them a month." Gail stared at Margaret harassing Christopher Brand and frowned. "Do me a favor, will you? Don't tell anybody her name is Margaret. She makes such a big *thing* out of being called Mrs. Harold until she asks somebody to use her Christian name. And believe me, it's her *Christian* name. I've been deliberately not telling anybody all day. Especially people like Christopher Brand, and Evelyn. God, who'd believe so many people would have such a hard time keeping their mouths shut?"

"I think it's part of the collective unconscious, or the primary material of DNA, or something," I said. "Can I tell Phoebe?"

"No. I only told you because I just couldn't stand it anymore. She gave Amelia Samson a little lecture on how she ought to be more careful to make sure her heroines got married by a minister. Or ministers. Whatever. And *Amelia* said—"

"I can just guess."

"Yeah, well. Margaret's a problem. Excuse me, Mrs. Keeley is a problem. And for some reason—don't ask me what—she's been worse than usual today."

"Worse than usual how?"

"Edgy, sort of. Combative. Of course, Mrs. Keeley is always combative. That's what she does with her life. But she's been—and that's weird, too, when I think about it. We came down to the station together in her car. And in the car, she was *better* than usual."

"What's better than usual?"

At the reception desk, Christopher Brand had (par for the course) done something to get Margaret Keeley's back up. She was haranguing him, pounding her right fist into the countertop, shaking her head vigorously. Christopher wasn't pounding, but his face had gone black. It was a scene almost calculated to make me nervous. There was something about Margaret Keeley that made her vulnerable to being trivialized. There was nothing like that about Christopher Brand. He looked murderous in the literal sense: as if, at any moment, he might reach out and snap Mrs. Keeley's neck in his hands.

Gail had been looking at them, too. Now she shuddered a little and turned her back to them.

"Scary, isn't he?" she said. "I didn't really know much about him when Evelyn asked me to give the party. Then I started hearing things. Did he really stab somebody? In a bookstore?"

"Evelyn told me he did," I said. "I *know* he went to jail once for beating up one of his wives. The Spanish painter one, I think."

"Well, I don't like him. And after I'd signed up for this thing, I went out and got one of his books, and I didn't like that either. Is that really what they're calling literature these days?"

"There's some talk they're going to give him a Nobel," I said. "On the other hand, he probably started it himself."

"Mmm. Well. It's too bad, you know. Because she really was better than usual this morning. All excited. I've noticed that at the store. You get these people who think they're sophisticated, and jaded, and God only knows what else, and you put them in front of a Real Live Author, and they turn to mush. I suppose it's different in New York. You've got writers everywhere there."

"Baltimore has Anne Tyler," I said. "God only knows, she's a better writer than Christopher Brand."

"Oh, we're used to Anne Tyler. We're impressed with her, but it isn't the same. I wish I knew what got Margaret started this morning. I'm telling you, everything was *fine*. And then we walked into the station, and we set up the table, and—"

"And what?"

Gail rubbed the side of her nose pensively. "I didn't realize it before. It was when she was talking to what's his name, the millionaire."

"Jonathon Hancock Lowry?"

"That's right. Everything was fine. Then the train came in, and people started to get off, and the first person who got off that I knew was Evelyn. And Evelyn was with this Jonathon Lowry. Anyway, I marched Mrs. Keeley over, and I introduced her, and everything was still fine. Then Evelyn and I went to fuss with the arrangements for the press conference. Then we came back, and Mrs. Keeley was talking to Jonathon Lowry—and she was like that. Edgy, like I said. Combative. Weird, isn't it?"

"The idea of Jon Lowry getting anyone upset is weirder than weird," I said. "The man's a mouse."

"Mmm. And hardly the last of the red-hot lovers or any of the other things that get Margaret upset. And he wasn't being rude. When I got over there, he was 'Mrs. Keeley-ing' her this and 'Mrs. Keeley-ing' her that. If any of her students gave her that kind of respect, she'd have an orgasm for a week."

"Do you use the word 'orgasm' around Mrs. Harold P. Keeley?" I said.

"Not when I'm thinking straight," Gail said. "That's Phoebe looking for you. You'd better go. I'll see you at four."

"Right," I said.

"Tell Phoebe to get some rest," Gail said. "She looks a little under the weather."

Gail clumped off in the direction of Mrs. Harold P. Keeley and Christopher Brand, and I started toward the end of the line and Phoebe.

# FOUR

What Christopher Brand and Mrs. Harold P. Keeley were arguing about wasn't morality, or profanity, or any of the other things I would have expected, but Mrs. Jenna Lee Haverman. Jenna Lee Haverman had been Christopher Brand's third wife, out of five or six. It was hard to keep track, because Christopher's "relationships" only lasted eight or nine months, and he didn't marry all of them. Even the ones he didn't marry had developed penchants for going to court. Palimony has provided not only a probably necessary protection for overly trusting women, but a window of opportunity for every world-class gold digger on earth. Christopher Brand had what amounted to a mania for gold diggers. He could have found one willing to marry him in a lesbian commune.

According to Mrs. Harold P. Keeley, Jenna Lee Haverman was *not* a gold digger—or hadn't been one until Christopher Brand turned her into one. When Mrs. Keeley got really angry, her voice turned into an air-raid-siren whine, sharp and hard and stabbing. Christopher's voice was a bass bellow, full of deep-throated rumblings that sounded very much like the thunder rolling by outside.

"Jesus *Christ,*" he said at one point, "that little bitch was a liar and a cheat from the day she was born."

"She was telling the truth," Margaret Keeley screeched. "She was telling the truth and any good lawyer could prove it."

"Telling the truth about what?" I asked Phoebe, as I propped her up next to the elevators. Phoebe was going into her nauseated-beyond-endurance state. Propping her up was necessary. If I hadn't, she probably would have fallen to the floor.

The elevators were in a bank in their own private hallway. If we'd moved down a few feet, we wouldn't have been able to see the reception desk at all. From where we were standing, we could see not only the desk but Christopher and Mrs. Keeley, too. Phoebe leaned over to get a better look and shook her head.

"As far as I can tell, Jenna Haverman went to some school Mrs. Keeley is connected with—"

"The Cardington School," I said.

"Whatever," Phoebe said. "Anyway, Mrs. Keeley's known her forever. And Mrs. Keeley says Jenna's a perfect little angel, and telling the absolute truth when she says she never signed a prenuptial agreement, and Christopher cheated her out of the alimony and settlement she *should* have had. And Christopher says—"

"I can guess what Christopher said," I said. "If it hadn't been for those prenuptial agreements, he'd have been broke by now."

"Especially with Jenna. She's the one he locked in the dog kennels all night in a blizzard or something. I don't remember. I do remember she got frostbite and lost four of her toes."

"Why didn't she sue him for damages?"

"I think she did. I think they won't let husbands and wives collect damages from each other. Or something."

"Peachy bird, our Great White Hope of American Literature."

"Well, *she's* peachy, too," Phoebe said. "She told me—" The blush spread over her face, and she turned to stare at the elevator doors, as if they could tell her something. They were very modern elevators. They wouldn't even tell her what floor they were on.

She kicked at the sides of them with the toe of her foot, sighing. "Did I see you pick something up at the reception desk? I thought I—"

"Yeah," I said. I rummaged around in my tote bag and came up with a plain white business envelope. "The clerk called me back just after you headed out here. Somebody left a message, I guess."

"Aren't you going to open it?"

"Why? It can't be from Nick or Adrienne. It wasn't mailed and it isn't a phone message. It had to have been hand-delivered. And you know what that means. Some fan who wants to tell me how he strangled his cat in the third grade."

"Yuck. Do they really tell you things like that?"

"All the time. They think I write about murders, I must get a kick out of murders. The gorier, the better."

"I write about sex. Nobody ever sends me letters about that. And even if it is from some nut, I think you should—"

Tempesta Stewart came chugging around the corner, carrying nothing but her six-inch-square, practically useless pocketbook. The woman didn't look entirely real. She dressed like a model in the kind of magazine that bills itself for "successful career women" and is really aimed at high-level secretaries and ambiguously titled "personal assistants." Her hair stuck out in unlikely places, but in the right unlikely places. Her makeup was as smooth and precise as if she'd put it on half a second before. She had come through a hailstorm after riding all night on a train, and her mascara wasn't even smudged.

She walked past Phoebe, punched at the up button and then folded her arms across her chest.

"If that elevator doesn't come in exactly thirty seconds, I'm going to take it apart," she said.

"I thought patience was a Christian virtue," I said.

She gave me a look. Then she gave Phoebe a look that traveled right down to the rise in Phoebe's belly, and made a face.

"I just can't spend any more time with that woman," she said. "She gives me the creeps. And don't start handing me a lot of crap about charity, because that woman wouldn't know charity if it walked right up and bit her. And don't start giving me a lot of crap about clichés, because—"

"Calm down," I said. "I wasn't going to give you any crap about anything."

"Why not? What makes today different from any other day?" She stabbed at the elevator button again. "Why I agreed to come on this tour, I don't know. Evelyn Nesbitt Kleig. Evelyn Nesbitt Kleig gives me the creeps. And this charity of hers—"

"You have something against helping the homeless?" Phoebe said.

"Helping the homeless? I've got nothing against helping the homeless. But this Ad Hoc Committee thing—had you ever heard of it before this trip?"

Mostly, Tempesta Stewart only asked rhetorical questions. She had no conversation, only techniques for putting her point across. For once, she looked honestly curious.

"All Evelyn's charities come up out of nowhere," I said. "You should know that by now. And they've all got those names, too. Ad Hoc Committee. Task Force. Whatever. It's the kind of thing that gets her attention."

"Well, I'm glad something does. Her work most surely doesn't. She ever run a tour for you?"

"Two," I said.

"Two," Tempesta repeated. "Two she's run for me, too. What am I saying? Anyway, they were a mess. An absolute mess. Charity is all well and good, but the Lord also wants us to do our jobs. That's what He gave us jobs *for.*"

"Right," I said.

"Don't give me that," Tempesta said. "At least Phoebe here understands religion. She practices a dead and discredited one, but at least she understands it."

"Did you really firebomb an abortion clinic in Nashville?" Phoebe said.

"Violence in defense of the unborn is no vice," Tempesta said. "And it wasn't an abortion clinic and I didn't firebomb it. It wasn't even in Nashville. It was in Montgomery and it was a Planned Parenthood referral office and all I did was set fire to the wastebasket. If it hadn't been for the *totally irrational* reaction of that idiotic nurse, it would never have gotten out of hand."

There was a freestanding ashtray on the other side of the hall, and no sign of the elevators, so I lit another cigarette. It occurred to me that I'd been smoking too much on this tour, and I smoked too much to begin with. My throat hurt.

"You notice something?" Tempesta said. "About the tour, I mean. We have hardly anything to do in Baltimore."

"You call an autograph party, a television show, a radio hour and four interviews nothing to do?" Phoebe said.

"Compared to what?" Tempesta said. "Compared to Minneapolis? In Minneapolis, I got less than two hours of sleep. Compared to Sherman Oaks? In Sherman Oaks, I got one, and it was right in that radio studio where we were doing the telethon thing. The microphone passed to someone else, and I just conked out. Now I've got nothing at all to do until four o'clock—three, if you count getting ready and getting over to that store—and tomorrow I've got this big hole in my schedule I'm going to have to fill talking to that woman's school."

"Evelyn probably realizes how exhausted we are," I said. "She isn't *that* bad at running a tour. We all look like death."

"Evelyn's a fanatic," Tempesta said, for all the world as if the one kind of person she couldn't stand was a fanatic. "If it was an ordinary book tour, I could see it. Evelyn never takes all that much interest in ordinary book tours. But this is for one of her charities. For heaven's sake, she could have set up three more parties in the time we have here."

"Be thankful for small favors," I said. "I've got a date with a room service menu and a bed. I'm going to keep it, too."

"You do what you want," Tempesta said. "I say there's too much crap going on around here. And talk about people giving me the creeps. I think that Jon Lowry is out to lunch."

"Well, at least you think he's out to somewhere in particular," I said.

The right-hand elevator hit the lobby, bouncing a little before its doors slid silently open. Tempesta put her hand against the rubber safety piece and stood back to let us get in ahead of her.

"You two think you're so smart," she said. "Just you wait."

I would have found out just what it was I should have been waiting for—Tempesta was like that; she abhorred innuendo, mostly because she also abhorred suspense—but just as we got into the car, two strangers appeared out of nowhere and got in with us. The strangers were two older men in business suits. Tempesta and Phoebe and I rode up to the fourth floor without speaking, washed by the sound of masculine voices talking about sales dips and cost-reduction strategies.

Unlocking our room, I found the bellboy had delivered our bags and whoever—probably a maid—had brought the three extra pillows and two extra blankets I had asked for at the desk. Since Phoebe always traveled with enough clothes to outfit the female half of one of old Mrs. Vanderbilt's Four Hundred parties, there were steamer trunks and suit bags everywhere, but no immediate sign of my single brown fabric suitcase or my little square makeup case. The makeup case is really my mother's, the one she used when she was a debutante in New York. I don't wear makeup often enough to justify buying one of my own.

I sat down on the bed closer to the window—and farther from the bathroom—and leaned over to extract the room service menu from the pile of service pamphlets on the night table. Phoebe rubbed her eyes, rubbed her forehead and headed for the john. That, of course, was when I should have done it—made an issue of it, demanded my explanations. Instead, I sat on the bed for long minutes, feeling utterly incapable of movement.

Tempesta had certainly been right about one thing: until Baltimore, the pace of the tour had been crazy. Crazed. My muscles felt like they were melting. My head was pounding. I rummaged around in my tote bag until I found my traveling clock—8:45. If I got to sleep *right that minute,* I'd be able to stay asleep for over six hours. On the other hand, there were things I had to do. Nick. Phoebe. Adrienne. I checked off the list in my head. I almost always called Adrienne as soon as I got into a new city, even if I had to call her at The Brearley School and haul her out of class to talk to her. Adrienne is a remarkable person, but a child whose mother has been murdered when she's old enough to understand what's going on, but not old enough to handle it, is never one hundred percent steady one hundred percent of the time. I liked letting her know where I was so she could get to me if she needed to, and I liked letting her know I was thinking of her. It was good for both of us. As for Nick . . . Lord, how I missed Nick.

As for Phoebe . . .

I got off the bed and went to the bathroom door. The sounds of retching were thick and awful, making me wince.

"Phoebe?" I said.

Thick cough. Muffled moan.

"Phoebe," I said again.

"I'm all right," Phoebe said.

"You don't sound all right."

"I am, really. It's just a little food poisoning, like I said. I don't need a doctor or anything. I'm just fine."

"If you have a little food poisoning, you're not fine."

"I am, really. Or I will be. Don't worry about it."

"That's like telling me not to be tall," I said. "Look. I'm dead tired. You must be, too. It would probably do you a lot of good if you got some sleep."

"I know."

"How long do you expect to be in there?"

"Patience—"

"Never mind," I sighed. My eyelids were getting heavy. I was finding it very difficult to stay on my feet. Psychology is a strange and wonderful thing. As long as I'd had places to go and work to do, I'd been exhausted but operational. My tiredness had been more like background music than an emergency. Now that I was within falling distance of a bed, whatever self-discipline I had—and it was never much—had deserted me.

I looked at the bed, broad and covered with blankets and pillows. I looked at something that might have been the corner of my suitcase peeking out from between two of Phoebe's trunks. I thought about the fact that I usually didn't like sleeping nude, but probably wouldn't mind this time. It had to beat dislodging my luggage.

"Phoebe?" I said again.

"I'm *all right,*" Phoebe said.

"I'm not," I said. "Listen. If I pass out *right this minute,* do you promise me you'll lie down and get some sleep as soon as you get out of there?"

"Patience, there is absolutely nothing in the world I want as much as I want to get some sleep."

"Good," I said.

"Lie down," she said. "You must be ready to collapse. You've been running around for hours. I'll be out of here in a minute."

"Okay."

The sounds of retching started up again. Phoebe was in trouble. Phoebe was my best friend. I had to do something about this.

The words had no force at all. I couldn't get them to connect with a course of action.

I went to the bed, lay down and tried not to close my eyes. I told myself to get up and get out of my clothes. I hate waking up after having slept in clothes. I told myself to rearrange the blankets and pillows. I love blankets and pillows. I told myself to set that damned traveling clock—all I needed was to sleep right through Gail Larson's meticulously planned champagne tea.

I drifted. At some point, I don't know when, Phoebe came into the room. She asked me the time. I mumbled something about the clock. She thanked me. I remember all that perfectly.

I don't remember anything else. I should have made myself stay awake. I should have done something about Phoebe. I should have set the alarm. Instead, I took the worst possible course of action.

I fell asleep.

# FIVE

When I was very young, my mother put a sign in my room, on the wall I faced when I sat up in bed, that said: "Effort Doesn't Count, Performance Does." It was one of those things—like Mrs. De Rham's dancing classes and spending Sunday mornings in a church built before the American revolution and my grandmother's coming-out pearls—that I never really thought about until I left home for Emma Willard, where a combination of scholarship students and the daughters of new-rich Texas wildcatters made me think the world might be something other than what I'd grown up believing it was. I even went through a period when I tried to make *myself* something other than I'd grown up believing I was. In fact, I went through several. There was my never-buy-anything-unless-it's-overpriced phase, nipped in the bud because my mother believed there was something sinful in giving any "child" under the age of eighteen an allowance of more than three dollars and fifty cents a week. There was my solidarity-with-the-people phase. That lasted longer—at least it was cheap—but the people I was trying to have solidarity with all thought I was crazy, and I began to feel uncomfortable. Finally, there was my expressing-my-real-feelings phase. That one lasted very long indeed, except that in a way it never got off the ground at all. I had it in conjunction with my I'm-a-woman-so-I-must-be-oppressed phase, and what it came down to was a lot of shouting about rage on the outside and a lot of feeling like a fool on the inside. I was seventeen years old, and it would be a long time before I understood that being discriminated against and being oppressed were not the same thing. Being a reasonably intelligent seventeen, I had the other two parts of the problem figured out right away. For one thing, expressing rage took a hell of a lot of work. For another: "Effort Doesn't Count. Performance Does."

I turned over in bed, confused. Somewhere a bell was ringing. I wasn't sure if it was in my dream or out. My dream was about building a jet plane. It was an epic, but it was a recurring epic. I'd had it on and off ever since college. These days, I had it most often when I had a deadline looming and didn't think I was going to make it. I was standing on a tall ladder next to a plane. The engine casing was open, exposing me to a lot of wires and metal I didn't understand the first thing about. A catalogue appeared in my hands, and I ordered every part in it, including the pink satin coat hangers. They came. They went into the engine. Nothing happened. I looked in and decided I'd had it all wrong. It was *used* parts I needed, something somebody else —somebody who *really understood* these things—had already found out would work. Another catalogue appeared in my hands and I ordered a few things from that one, only the absolutely necessary things. When they came they were rusty and dull and fell apart in my hands. I dropped them on the ground—or what was left of them after whole sections had scattered into flakes of rust—and turned my attention to the power of my emotions. They were mostly negative. They were no work at all. They had not one single effect on that jet engine. "Effort Doesn't Count. Performance Does."

There wasn't *a bell* ringing. There were two. I sat up in bed, squinting in the darkness. Phoebe must have drawn the curtains. I didn't remember doing it, and they were pulled solidly over the broad windows. Outside, I could hear the sounds of rain and wind, violent and blank.

Phoebe. Where was Phoebe?

I looked at the opposite bed, empty except for a pile of velvet caftans and a little jumble of matching string bags. I listened for bathroom sounds. There was nothing. I was alone.

I reached for my cigarettes with one hand and the phone with another, called out "Just a minute" to whoever had been ringing my bell and was now pounding on my door, put the receiver to my ear and said, "Hello?"

"McKenna?" Nick said. "McKenna, is that you? Are you all right?"

"Nick," I said. "Just a minute. Somebody's at the door."

I got out of bed and headed toward the miniature entrance foyer, thankful that I had fallen asleep in my clothes. I felt gritty and wet with sweat, but at least I didn't have to search around for something to wear. I am not good at waking up, in the morning or at any other time. I need three cups of coffee and half a dozen cigarettes just to remember where I keep my panty hose, and I've kept them in the third drawer of whatever dresser I've owned since I was sixteen years old. I stumbled over one of Phoebe's trunks. They had been scattered all over the room—God, I must have been out cold—and this one had been opened. Bits of veiling and odd-shaped lengths of imitation fox fur drooled out of it. Phoebe was the neatest packer I had ever met. She made my mother's look a mess, and my mother's would put a Marine DI into terminal orgasm. What *was* this?

I opened the door and peered out into the hall at Jon Lowry, looking sheepishly in the general direction of his shoes.

"Damn," I said. "Whoever heard of bells on hotel doors?"

"It wasn't a bell," Jon said. "It was this."

He held up a little black box, a kind of miniature VCR remote. When he punched at the only button on it, it buzzed.

"I bought it in Times Square," he said. "It's really very handy when you want to—when you don't want to—you know. When you're at a door that doesn't have a bell and you don't want to knock and make a lot of noise."

"You *did* knock and make a lot of noise."

I stood back and let him inside, ignoring his comment about the darkness and his three separate, and increasingly elaborate, apologies for waking me up. I went back to the bed, picked up the phone again and switched on the night-table light. Underneath it was my traveling clock, its green luminous hands fading in the sudden brightness. It said 3:15.

"Crap," I said.

"McKenna?" Nick said.

"Sorry," I said. "I overslept. I meant to get up by three and call you."

"Call me where?"

My cigarettes were next to the traveling clock. I wormed one out of the pack and reached for my lighter. Jon Lowry sat down on the chair in front of the vanity table on the other side of the room, being careful to move the pile of Phoebe's pure silk half slips to the top of the dresser first. I got my cigarette lit. I found an ashtray. I counted to ten.

"Start again," I said. "Where would I call you? It's three o'clock in the afternoon. I'd call you at your office."

"I'm at the train station," Nick said. "In Baltimore."

"What?"

"McKenna, I'm *supposed* to be at the train station in Baltimore. I mean, we had a little trouble, we're late. I'm supposed to be at the hotel. But I'm not supposed to be at my office, and you know it."

"What are you doing in Baltimore? Why should I know it?"

"I was right, wasn't I?" Adrienne's voice in the background. "She was asleep when we talked to her in St. Louis. She doesn't remember a thing about it."

"I was not asleep when I talked to you from St. Louis," I said. "I remember that conversation distinctly."

"The first one or the second one?" Nick said.

"Oh, shit," I said.

"Never mind," Nick said. "We're here. Just the two of us. Adrienne wanted to bring Courtney Feinberg, and I like Courtney Feinberg, but you know how they get—"

I grunted. I certainly knew how they got. The Brearley School, where I'd sent Adrienne after she came to live with me, is supposed to be the best girls' school in New York. If "best" was to be translated as "school with the most intelligent students," and Adrienne and Courtney were anything like typical, I'd have to give Brearley that. The problem is, two hyper-intelligent eight-year-olds can be a menace, especially when they really like each other. Adrienne and Courtney really liked each other. Over the past year, they had: found a way to travel through the theoretically sealed-off dumbwaiter system in my apartment building; rigged a pulley-and-basket contraption that effectively brought Girl Scout cookies from the cabinet in the kitchen to the bedroom at the end of the back hall Adrienne now called her own; and used the cat in an experiment that had something to do with kites and the penthouse garden. I had absolutely no idea what I was going to do with the two of them when they got old enough to think about sex.

I tapped ash into the ashtray and sighed. "Well," I said, "no Courtney Feinberg is a start in the right direction. What are you two doing here?"

"Keeping you sane at that party," Nick said.

"Well, I'll probably need that."

"We thought you would. And we got here. But the weather's awful, and since Adrienne says she can change in the ladies' room—"

"Change into what?"

"I bought her a new party dress. A jumper thing. That kind of material Phoebe always wears. Adrienne's is—"

"Old rose," Adrienne said from the background.

"God," Nick said. "I had no idea children's clothes were so expensive."

I stared at the ceiling and contemplated serious liquor, right in the middle of the afternoon. That was another thing about Adrienne and Courtney Feinberg. Left without proper supervision, they tended to drift to the Miss Dior section of the children's department.

"Anyway," Nick said. "I've got the address, I thought we'd go right over to that store. We've only got the one overnight bag. Gail can store it behind a desk for us or something. She must have a desk."

"I'm sure she does," I said.

"So. We'll see you there. It's a good thing we came, anyway. I've got a couple of things I want to talk over with you."

"What things?"

"McKenna, trust me. I can't explain on the phone. Things have been weird. You got a letter from the IRS that doesn't make any sense at all. David's disappeared. It's been crazy."

"Wait," I said.

"See you in an hour," Nick said.

*"Nick,"* I said.

The phone went to dial tone in my hand.

I stared at the receiver for a moment and then slammed it into the cradle.

At the vanity table, Jon Lowry arranged his face in an expression of polite obliviousness and folded his hands in his lap. I'd never seen a man fold his hands in his lap before. He reminded me of the punks you see on buses in London. They look like exactly the sort of people you'd run a mile from if you met them on the street in New York, and they're all as polite as good little boys being shown off at a grandmother's tea party.

Jon Lowry looked like a mall-arcade video-game nerd. He dressed like one, too. Complete control of eight hundred fifty million dollars had excited in him no lust for material possessions, and none of the kind of vanity that can be indulged by throwing wads of money in the direction of make-over spas, personal trainers and the custom department of Brooks Brothers Manhattan store. His nose was almost as big as his Adam's apple, and his Adam's apple was huge. His hair looked like he'd cut it himself. His clothes might have been the result of a solidarity-with-the-people phase, but I didn't think so. What I thought was that, Jon being Jon, he probably hated shopping even more than he hated large groups of people. His sneakers were ancient Nikes, held together with electrical tape. His jeans were plain Levi's and patched with calico squares. His denim jacket was clean but worn. He'd probably bought the whole outfit just after being let loose into the world, and not recovered from the experience yet. His Dr. Who T-shirt was brand-new, but he could have bought that off a souvenir stand in Manhattan without ever having to try it on.

My cigarette was out. I lit another one, ran my free hand through my hair and waited. It was impossible to start a conversation with Jonathon Hancock Lowry. The harder you tried, the faster he backpedaled.

He unclasped his hands. He stared at his shoes. He looked at the ceiling. Finally, he started clearing his throat: a good sign.

"So," he said. "So. I guess—Phoebe isn't here?"

"Phoebe isn't here," I agreed. "But don't ask me where she is. I've been asleep."

"I want to apologize for waking you up," he said. "I really do. I had no idea—"

"The phone started ringing when you did," I pointed out.

He brightened. "That's right. It did. I don't have to—Evelyn keeps trying to teach me all about moral relativity, and I think I understand it, but I just get so confused—"

"Evelyn is trying to teach you about moral relativity?"

"Evelyn is a very unusual person," he said. "Really. She's so dedicated. And so *strong.* She went out with me the very first time I asked her. And she didn't even know who I *was.* "

"Mmm," I said.

"Even after she knew who I was, she didn't want me to buy her things. I keep giving her presents and she won't take them. She wants to put everything into charities. My mother was like that."

"I thought your mother died when you were two."

"She did. They both did. My father, too. But Aunt Gertrude used to tell me about them. When she wasn't telling me about—other things."

"Like how the world was full of people trying to kidnap you?"

"She meant well," Jon said. "She was just paranoid. I mean really paranoid. After I came into the money, the doctor sat down and had a talk with me, and what *he* said was if she hadn't had control of my trust, she'd have been locked away years ago. There's some medical name for it—"

"The popular name is paranoid schizophrenia. I think that will do."

"Yeah. Well. I didn't have her locked up. She may have been crazy, but she was happy crazy. And then a couple of years later she had a stroke anyway, so it didn't matter. She died. And Evelyn's right. No matter what it looked like at the time, it wasn't my fault."

"The stroke wasn't your fault?" I asked in confusion.

"Yeah. I mean, when I did it, the lawyers said my *father* would have had a stroke about the money, and it took a ten-ton truck to kill him. And so I thought—"

"What did you do about the money?"

"Do?"

"Jon—"

"Yeah. You see, I didn't exactly do something. I didn't do something. When the money came to me, they liquidated all the investments— they had to, it was that way in the will—and then I was supposed to reinvest them. Only I didn't."

"You have eight hundred fifty million dollars that's not invested in anything?"

"Well, some of it's in gold. In fact, a lot of it is. And some of it's in the house in Weston, you know, and my apartment in the city. But most of it's in safety deposit boxes—you're going to have a stroke, too."

A stroke was hardly the word for it. I know very little about money. I have no talent for it, and even less interest. I had, however, got to that point in my life where people insisted on explaining it to me. I had absorbed a few of the more basic details. The cardinal rules were these: First, you used money to make money. Second, you *never* dipped into capital. I tried to think what Nick would do if I wanted to keep the money from even one of my royalty payouts—less than a hundred thousand dollars—in a safety deposit box. I came up with a mental image of thermonuclear war.

"It makes more sense than you think it does," Jon said defensively.

"If you've got eight hundred fifty million dollars, you should be able to do anything you want with your life."

"What can you *possibly* do with money in safety-deposit boxes you couldn't do with it earning interest?"

"Not file income tax."

My mouth dropped open.

"People don't realize," Jon said. "You know, if you make any money at all in this country, you might as well tear up the Constitution and throw it away. The government gets to try you in tax court as guilty until proven innocent. You can have your property seized with no notice at all. They can search through your files without telling you they're doing it. They can even search through your house. And you know what they say? They say following the Constitution would make it too hard for the government to collect its money. And the courts let them get away with it, too. The courts say the government's right to take your money is more important than any right of any kind you think you have. And you know further what? King George said that, too, except it was about the Magna Carta or whatever, and it was after he said that that John Adams decided to come over to the side of the American revolution. John Adams thought it was the most terrible thing he'd ever heard. He thought it was tyranny. And he was right."

"But—" I said.

"I had a great-great-great-grandfather who *fought* in the revolution," Jon said.

"But," I said again.

"And the Bill of Rights makes it hard to convict murderers, too. I mean, if they were going to tear up the whole American idea and throw it in the wastebasket, wouldn't you think they'd do it over the Son of Sam?"

My cigarette had gone out again, not burned down but just gone out. I relit it, put my lighter back on the night table, and started shaking my head.

"I think you've got to be missing something," I said. "I think—"

"I'm not missing anything," Jon said. "You think about it for a while. You get in trouble with the IRS just once, even with an honest mistake. Hell, you know what started me on this? I discovered a tax fraud and I went to report it. I just walked right into this IRS office in Greenwich and tried to do the right thing. I got treated like Al

Capone. And it went on for *three years*. Now I don't even have a social security number, or not one I have to use, anyway. As long as I don't knock off some little old lady, I'm free. And it wasn't true what they said about somebody stealing it."

"Wasn't true what who said?"

"The lawyers," Jon said patiently. "They said keeping all that money in demand accounts—that's when your money is somewhere and you can get it right out just by asking for it—anyway, they said if I kept it in demand accounts somebody could steal it, even if it made interest. That's why I used the safety-deposit boxes, and the gold. Of course, when I die, whoever gets it will have to—"

"I'm surprised they didn't have you locked up," I said.

"If they couldn't get Gertrude locked up, they certainly couldn't get me locked up. Do you know when Phoebe's coming back? I was supposed to help her out with something but then Evelyn wanted to show me around Baltimore and we got a little held up, so I was late, and then—"

"Evelyn wanted to show you around Baltimore?"

"She's from Baltimore. I thought you knew that."

"For some reason I thought she was from New York," I said.

"And it's three-thirty now," Jon said. "Don't you have to—do something to yourself before the party?"

Three-thirty. I levered myself off the bed. It takes me half an hour just to figure out what to do with my makeup.

At the far end of the little entrance foyer, there was a scratching and a churning and a clanking of gears. The door swung open. The sound of feet shuffling on a carpet melted into the sound of a slam.

A moment later, Phoebe appeared in the room, looked at both of us in turn and burst into tears.

# SIX

Most of the same people who think romance writers are stupid also think they're overemotional, empty-headed ninnies who cry—or collapse into dead faints—at the smallest possible provocation. The truth was, I'd seen Phoebe cry only once or twice in all the years I'd known her, and her tears hadn't been the histrionic kind. A slight watering. A suggestion of red at the rims of the eyelids. Even over the last few weeks, when pregnancy might have explained theatrics, it had never been more than that. You do not go from a half-slum in a dying industrial town in New Jersey to ten rooms on Central Park West by being empty-headed *or* hysterical. If Phoebe had burst into tears, I had to assume she had some *reason* to.

Unfortunately, I was still half asleep. My brain was working through all this very slowly. Phoebe's brain was working through whatever it was working through at the speed of light. By the time I had decided that this was serious, not hormonal, she had sized up the situation in the room, turned her back on us and slammed another door. That door muffled the sound of her continued crying. Jonathon and I seemed to be sitting in a silent, echoing space. What echoed most loudly were the scrape and click of the bathroom door's bolt being thrown.

My mental gears were even more sluggish than I'd thought they'd been. It wasn't until then, when I knew she had locked herself away from me, that I realized why she'd looked so odd when she came in: she wasn't in her Phoebe Damereaux costume. I thought back, trying to concentrate. Big brown tent dress. Shapeless brown coat. Espadrilles. Back in the days when she was a fat, poor girl in a thin, rich girls' college, she'd dressed that way all the time—whether out of carelessness or hopelessness, I never knew. It had been years since I'd seen her in anything similar. For public occasions, she had the caftans. For lying around at home, she had three dozen monk's-robe-style terry-cloth robes. For going out to dinner with friends she had tent dresses that had been made for her in the custom department of Saks, and looked it. And she *never* stepped outside in cold weather without one fur or another over her shoulders. I hadn't even known she owned a cloth coat.

I tried to put it all together and couldn't. She had been out, that had been obvious. Not only had she been wearing a coat, but I had the vague impression that her hair had been wet. She looked just as tired as she had when we'd first walked into the room, which meant she probably hadn't been to sleep. I gave a quick look at the traveling clock: 3:42. It had been almost seven hours. Where in the name of God could Phoebe have gone, in a city she knew nothing about, for *seven hours?*

"Oh God," Jon Lowry said.

I looked up to find him standing next to the vanity table, looking as stricken as a drunk driver who'd just run into a dog.

"I better go talk to her," he said. "This is all my fault. I promised to—"

"Get out of here," I said.

"What?"

"Get out of here. Now. Go. She'll talk to you later."

"But you don't understand," he said. "I was supposed to—"

"Whatever you were supposed to do, you didn't do," I said. "And it doesn't matter now. Believe me. I have a fair idea of what this is about. It couldn't possibly have anything to do with you."

"Miss McKenna," Jon said, "you just don't—"

"Out," I said again.

I got up, crossed the room to him and got him by the collar of his jacket. I'd read new-wave female-private-eye novels where the heroine is always beating up on the bad guys. I'd found them completely untenable. I'm a physically larger woman than most. I didn't think I could beat up on anybody, not bare-handed. I beat up on Jonathon Hancock Lowry nonetheless. I got him away from the vanity table. I got him through the entrance foyer. I got him into the hall. Whether that was my strength, my emotions, or Jon's innate politeness, I'll never know. I doubt if it matters anyway.

He stood in the hall with his hands in the pockets of his jeans. "Patience," he said, "if you'd just let me explain."

"Later."

"But I think I may—"

"Later," I insisted. The truth was, if Phoebe *had* told Jon something she hadn't told me, especially about this, I didn't want to know about it. I was going to have a hard enough time doing what I had to do as it was.

"See you at the party," I said. "We'll be late."

Then I closed the door in his face.

I stood in the foyer for a while, looking into the half-lit gloom. The curtains seemed to be closed on perfect exterior blackness. If there were streetlamps out there, or floodlights for the portico at the hotel's front door, their light didn't reach us. The only light that did came from the night-table lamp I'd turned on when I first woke. All that came from the bathroom were intermittent eruptions of tears and heaving.

I put my forehead against the bathroom door and said, "Phoebe?"

"Go away."

"No."

"Go *away*. I'm fine. I'm getting dressed."

"Your clothes are all out here."

"I've got the green caftan in here. I'm getting dressed."

"You wore the green caftan on the train. You had the red cleaned for the party tonight. It's out here. Come and get it."

"If you don't go away, I'm never going to speak to you again."

"If you're not out of there in thirty seconds, I'm going to get Amelia to break down this door."

"Shit," Phoebe said.

"I don't see why I should care if you stop speaking to me anyway," I said. "You haven't been for the past three weeks."

Footsteps on tile, the metal whine of a bolt retracting: the door swung slowly open, and Phoebe stuck her head out. She looked awful. Her hair wasn't wet. It was that gritty-dull matte hair gets when it has dried after being drenched with sweat. She was wearing no makeup. She usually wore a lot. She almost never needed it. At that moment, she needed it the way Al Capone had needed a good tax lawyer.

Al Capone. Tax lawyers. I still had Jonathon Hancock Lowry wandering around in my head someplace.

I stepped back and let Phoebe come past me. She edged along the wall until she got to the room. Then she walked carefully to the bed she'd claimed as her own—the one with the piles of clothes on it—and sat down.

"I'm pregnant," she said.

"I know," I said.

"I thought you might," she said. "I suppose it's been obvious."

"Obvious? Why? Just because you've been throwing up every ten seconds since we left New York and you look like you've gained fifty pounds?"

"Patience—"

"Phoebe, I'm sorry. Don't cry. But for God's sake, we tell each other everything. The first time you ever slept with David you called me up while he was in the bathroom to tell me you'd—I just don't understand why you haven't *said* anything."

"David," Phoebe said.

"You've been driving me crazy," I said.

Phoebe's eyes filled with tears. Her breath began to come in great, gulping hitches, as if there would never be enough air. "Oh God," she said. "David. You'll tell David, won't you? Tell him that I tried? Because I did try, I really did. I went all the way down there, I really did, and then when I got to the place I—but I did try. I really did. And I understand—"

"Tried what?" I said. "Understand what?"

Phoebe flushed. "I tried," she repeated. "You know. I tried to get it aborted."

I sat straight down on the floor. It should have hurt. I didn't feel a thing. "What did you say?"

*"I tried to get it aborted,"* she exploded. Then she leaped to her feet and started pacing, furious, the old Phoebe, unhampered by hormones or lack of sleep. "He told me to get it done and I thought about it. I thought about it the whole three weeks. And I—I love him. I really do. I love him more than I've ever loved anybody except maybe my mother. And I understand this. I know what he's worried about. I don't even blame him. So in St. Louis I decided I'd get it done here. I mean, he has reason on his side, Pay, he really does. So—you know those phone books Evelyn carries around with her all the time?"

"I think so."

"She's got one for every city on the tour. So she can phone ahead for things. Anyway, I borrowed the Baltimore one and got a referral from Planned Parenthood and then I—I made an appointment. Not with Planned Parenthood but with the clinic they gave me the name of. The doctor. I don't know. Anyway, I explained the whole thing sort of and I made the appointment for today because I thought I'd— I'd get it done and then I'd have the party to take my mind off it and all the interviews and things—"

"We don't have all that many interviews in Baltimore, Phoebe."

"We have some," she insisted. "And it would be better than having it in New York and then being at home and everything. Well. You went to sleep and I went there. I did. I went."

"And?"

"I couldn't do it. I don't want to do it. I *won't* do it."

"Okay," I said. "Don't get hysterical. You didn't do it. It's all right."

"No, it's not."

"Why?"

"Because when David finds out about it, he's going to leave me."

"Jesus Christ," I said. "When Nick finds out about this, David isn't going to have to leave you, because David is going to be dead. How can you defend that son of a—"

"Patience, I'm more pregnant than you think I am. Nearly five months."

"So?"

"So, I had one of those—what do you call them? With the needle. Amnio—"

"Amniocentesis."

Phoebe brightened. "He's a boy." Her face fell again. "He's got that thing—spina bifida."

"Oh *Lord.*" I leaned back until I was touching the wall and blew a stream of breath into the air. "Oh, Phoebe, I'm sorry."

"I'm sorry, too. But not so sorry I want to kill him."

"Is that how you think of it, killing him?"

"There are people who say they know before they ever have to make a decision. Tempesta. All those nurses at that clinic. I don't think that's true. I think you have to be here. And I *am* here and I *do* think it would be killing him. And I'm not going to change my mind about it *no matter what.*"

I leaned forward again. "Throw me my cigarettes," I said. "You don't have to change your mind about it. If it makes you feel any better, I'm not deliriously happy with that particular activity myself."

"I looked up spina bifida," Phoebe said. "And it's not so simple. It's not like I know already he's going to be a vegetable or die a couple of days after he's born. He could just have a mild case and be fine once they did a little fixing up. He could be physically handicapped but okay otherwise. There's that big physicist at Harvard who has that genetic muscle disease and has to be in a wheelchair, but he's going to get a Nobel Prize anyway. It doesn't make any *sense* to me to kill him because he's sick and maybe it'll take a lot of time and money to take care of him. It doesn't make any *sense*. If I had him already, I wouldn't do that. I think of that Baby Doe case where they let that child starve to death just because she was retarded and I want to—I want to—he's my *Benjamin*."

"Benjamin Damereaux?"

"Benjamin Weiss. It was going to be Benjamin Weiss Grossman, but—"

"Throw me my cigarettes," I said again.

She got my cigarettes off the night table and threw them randomly into the air. I had to crawl across half a foot of carpet to get to them. When I sat back down, I saw that Phoebe had begun to gather up pieces of her Damereaux costume.

"We'd better go," she said. "We're supposed to be there already."

"Could you tell me one thing?" I asked her. "It couldn't have taken you six or seven hours just to go to an abortion clinic and walk right out again. What were you doing?"

She shrugged. "Walking around. It took me about half an hour to get there, and then I sat in the waiting room for a while. Read pamphlets. Got sick. Then I just sort of drifted. I took a couple of buses. And I kept running into people. It was like fate or God or something. I was walking around this good-sized city I'd never been in before, and everywhere I went I ran into people I knew. I mean, I know we all came here together, but—"

"Who did you run into?"

"What? Oh, Evelyn and Jon Lowry. Holding hands, yet. They were on the other side of the street, so I didn't have to do anything to keep them from seeing me. I think they were going into some kind of museum. And Tempesta was sitting in the front room of this storefront building, the American Army for Christ the King. And Christopher Brand was coming out of a bank. And then there was that woman, Mrs. Harold P. Keeley." Phoebe made a face. "I had to duck behind a No Parking sign to make sure she didn't see me. I wasn't in the mood to talk to anybody, but *her*—"

"I don't blame you."

"I don't think she has any children. I think she ate her young. And I really had to worry about her, too, because she was looking for somebody. She kept checking her watch and peering into the distance and making these little clucking noises at the back of her throat. *Are* you going to get dressed?"

"In a second. Tell me one more thing. Did you tell Jon Lowry about any of this?"

"Jon Lowry? No, of course not. Why would I?"

"He came up here saying he'd promised to do something for you. And then you burst into tears and he said it was all his fault."

"Oh, that." Phoebe reached to the floor and picked up her purse, the leather one she used when she was being, as she put it, "an ordinary person." She fumbled through it until she came up with a manila envelope. She threw the manila envelope in my lap. "There," she said. "That's what that's all about. He probably thought I'd lost it and got all upset."

"What is it?"

"Money."

I opened the envelope and looked inside. There was indeed money. There was, in fact, a great deal of money. I dumped it onto the floor and started counting fifty-dollar bills. When I got to three thousand without making a dent in the pile, I stopped.

"He's nuts," I said.

"Fifty thousand five hundred," Phoebe said. "And as far as I'm concerned, he *is* nuts. I think he does everything in cash. Anyway, he asked me to hold it for him this morning, and he was supposed to come get it around one. I take it he was late."

"By a couple of hours."

"Can you imagine someone rich enough to be a couple of hours late picking up fifty thousand dollars in *cash?*"

"I think I agree with his lawyers. He ought to be committed. We have to give that back."

Phoebe shrugged. "He'll be at the party. We will be, too, if you'd hurry up. I'm surprised you're not dressed already. You haven't seen Nick in three weeks. And Adrienne."

I stuffed the money back into the envelope and got to my feet.

Apparently, I was the only person on earth who didn't remember Nick's second phone call to me in St. Louis.

# SEVEN

Gail Larson's mystery bookstore, The Butler Did It, sits in the middle of a block on North Charles Street distinguished chiefly for its contradictory architecture. Most of the buildings, like the one whose first floor is taken up by The Butler Did It itself, are converted row houses. The row houses each have two tall windows facing the street, and what we in New York would call stoops. I don't think "stoops" was the word for them in Baltimore. The street had started out to be too elegant for stoops, all brick facing and graceful curving latticework. The occupants of the row houses were evidently attempting to keep it that way. They were fighting an uphill battle. It's difficult keeping a block elegant when the middle of one side of it is taken up by a gas station, which this one's was. It's even more difficult in the face of the existence of something that calls itself the Elite VIP Lounge. I looked out the window of the cab and wondered who I'd root for. I understood the aspirations of the row-house people. City real estate is expensive to buy and even more expensive to maintain. Existing "good" neighborhoods are almost always beyond the reach of the urban-oriented young middle class. On the other hand, I have a real weakness for bars like the Elite VIP Lounge. They're definitely the best places to get drunk in, and they *always* have great jukeboxes. Kenny Rogers doing "The Gambler." Tammy Wynette doing "D*I*V*O*R*C*E." Linda Ronstadt doing any one of a hundred songs that make the course of true love sound like a bed of nails. In a world where all popular music seems to be performed by twelve-year-olds herding together to found tone-deaf bands called "The Entrails of Satan's Cat," there is a real need for places like the Elite VIP Lounge.

The storm that had started out as wind and sleet that morning had turned to snow: gentler, but no easier to drive through. Our cab came to a sliding stop in front of the six-foot-tall butler sign that hung before the store's two windows, and the driver cursed. Then he looked at us in the rearview mirror with the same expression he'd had on his face when he'd picked us up at the hotel. To say he wasn't sure he wanted us in his cab was putting it mildly. He thought we were nuts. If Phoebe hadn't been so short, he would have suspected her of being a transvestite.

If Phoebe hadn't been so short and so *pregnant*. Now that I knew— or maybe I should say knew I knew—I was no longer surprised that Tempesta Stewart had guessed. I wasn't surprised that the cabdriver had guessed. There is only one condition that gives that particular kind of roundness to a face, or turns a woman all those odd colors. I reached into my pocket and found a handful of saltines.

"Here," I said. "You're going green again."

"Those aren't working, Patience. They're really not."

"Eat them anyway."

"You want to pay up and get out before one of those drunks dents my cab?"

I dug into my tote bag and came up with my wallet. The drunks in question were not denizens of the Elite VIP Lounge. *Those* people all had sense enough to stay in out of the snow and a windchill factor that must have brought the temperature down to about twenty degrees. *These* people belonged to the party at The Butler Did It. They were all carrying little plastic champagne glasses. They had ditched their coats somewhere inside. They slid up and down the steps leading up to TBDI's front door in silks and fine winter wools. All of them looked cold.

I popped the door, got out onto the street and held back for Phoebe. She stuck her nose into the air and surveyed the scene.

"They must have been early," she said. "They couldn't have gotten into this condition in only an hour."

"I don't see why not," I said.

"Do you see Nick and Adrienne?"

"The only person I see that I know is Jon Lowry. He doesn't look happy."

Phoebe slid onto the sidewalk—it's hard to do anything but slide out of a car when you're wearing a floor-length dyed-white chinchilla cape —and peered into the crowd. Jon Lowry was at the top of the steps, on just this side of the door. He looked depressed enough to commit suicide.

"I wonder what's wrong with him," Phoebe said, as if she didn't care.

"Maybe it's the money," I told her.

She checked her bag, found the envelope and nodded. "We'll be able to cheer him up, then. I wish I could see Nick, though. I *really, really* want to talk to Nick."

I said, "Mmm." Around the time we'd asked the doorman at the Sheraton Inner Harbor to get us a cab, I'd remembered something: Nick telling me that David Grossman had "disappeared." I hadn't told Phoebe about it because I hadn't wanted to upset her any more than she already was. She had managed to get control of herself, but the tears and hysteria were still just beneath the surface. Still, it worried me. First he tells her he wants her to have an abortion. Then he takes off without a word to anybody. I knew Nick. Nick never panicked, or jumped to conclusions, or used words carelessly. Law school had drummed both cautiousness and precision into his very bones. If he said David Grossman had disappeared, that was exactly what he meant. Not that he simply couldn't find the man. Not that David had missed an appointment or forgotten to keep a date for lunch. I wondered what the hell was going on.

*Wonder about Jon Lowry,* I told myself. *That's at least something you can do something about.*

I grabbed Phoebe's arm and started to guide her up the steps, moving slowly so that she didn't topple off her shoes. Like too many short women, Phoebe absolutely insists on wearing four-inch spikes whenever she has to be in the company of tall people. Since I am definitely a tall person, and since she's almost always in my company, she wears four-inch spikes almost all the time. Even under her bathrobes.

"We're going to have to go out and get you some new shoes," I said.

"Phoebe," Jon Lowry said. "Miss McKenna. Do you know where Evelyn is?"

It was like that old actor's dream about going onstage only to find yourself appearing in the wrong play. Neither Phoebe nor I could think of a single thing to say. Evelyn. Money. Envelopes. Evelyn. It just didn't make sense.

It made sense to Jon, the wrong kind.

"Damn," he said. "I was sure she was with you. You were so late, I figured she must be chasing you around. To be sure you got here."

"She's not here?" I said, and thought: *stupid.*

"She hasn't been yet. God, Gail Larson is tearing her hair out. I'm serious. There's all this stuff—book boxes and pens. I don't know. Stuff that was supposed to be done to set up. And none of it got done. And you know Evelyn. She gets a little distracted sometimes, but she doesn't not show up."

"I've got your envelope," Phoebe said. She took it out of her purse and handed it to him.

Jon Lowry said, "Oh," folded it up and stuck it into the loose waistband of his jeans. He would have been more worried about the fate of a dozen Watchmen comics than he was about all that money.

I edged past him and looked into the store. It wasn't as packed as it had seemed from the street, but it was pretty full. The only entirely empty corner in the place seemed to be around the table in the back. It was covered with a blue linen tablecloth that reached to the floor and equipped with pens, plastic champagne glasses, ashtrays and two little piles of cigarette boxes: Marlboros for Christopher Brand, Carltons for me. Obviously, this was where Gail had intended to have authors sign books. Instead, the authors were scattered into every other corner of the oversized room. So were the books. I caught sight of a pile of *Blood Red Romance,* hardcover edition, near a little display of the complete works of Dorothy L. Sayers.

The authors weren't all that hard to find. Amelia had established herself near the Raymond Chandlers and was holding court, assisted by both Hazel Ganz and Lydia Wentward. Christopher Brand had been backed into a corner by a blousy woman in a synthetic green satin dress cut down to her navel. His square jaw was working compulsively, as if he were chewing a cud. Tempesta Stewart was sitting on Gail Larson's checkout desk, giving a little lecture to a group of desperately respectable-looking young women who nodded frantically at every word she said. I looked around a little more and found Nick and Adrienne, stuck behind a pair of fat men engaged in something just one step away from a physical fight. They jabbed forefingers in the air and into each other's chests. Adrienne's dress was beautiful. I revised my estimate of just how much she'd talked Nick out of upward, to at least a hundred fifty dollars.

Nick saw me, smiled, pointed at the two fat men and shrugged. I shrugged back and waved.

Phoebe ducked under my arm and into the store. "There they are. Maybe I should go rescue them."

"Maybe you should," I said. "I'll try to find Gail and see if I can help."

"I'm right here."

I looked behind me to find Gail struggling with a large box marked AST—BLOOD. I took it out of her hands. It was heavy enough to kill somebody.

Gail brushed blond hair out of her face. "Thank God you're here. You don't *know* what I've been going through. It would be one thing if all these people were mystery writers. I'd probably have had enough books to get started. Instead, they're all sorts of things and I didn't have any of the books on the floor but yours, and you weren't here."

"The books didn't show up?" This was a common problem with signings. For some reason, it is impossible to explain to any publisher's shipping department that an autograph party without books for an author to autograph doesn't quite cut it.

That, however, was not Gail's problem. "The books are here," she said. "They're just in the ballroom. In boxes. Not even very well-marked boxes. And on top of that, there are other boxes, and somehow everything got all mixed in together. I'm having the worst time sorting it out. And in the meantime—"

"You're not selling anything."

"I'm selling my hind end off. You have no *idea* how many people are delighted to realize that Agatha Christie is still in print."

"Does that money go to charity?" I asked.

"It's going to have to. I made a little mistake in the ad I ran in the *Sun.*" She tapped the box I was carrying. "Go take that over to the table, sit down, open up and start signing books. I'll go back to the office and try to find the rest of them. And when I get my hands on Evelyn Nesbitt Kleig—"

"She'll probably have an explanation, you know," I said. "Jon Lowry's right, she's a flake, but she's a responsible flake. Especially when it comes to her charities. Whatever's holding her up, it's got to be unavoidable."

"I don't care if she was spirited away by elves," Gail said. "I'm having a nervous breakdown."

She turned on her heel and stomped away. At my side, Phoebe stirred a little and said, "I think I'm going to be sick. Again."

"Don't be," I said. "There's no place for you to be sick in. Go get Nick and Adrienne. I'm going to take this box over to the desk and get us started. If Tempesta goes for me, fight her off."

"Why would Tempesta go for you?"

"She always likes to sign first. Remember New Orleans?"

"Oh," Phoebe said. "Yeah. But Christopher Brand is smarter, you know. He always likes to sign last."

"And he always loses out to Amelia. Go get Nick and Adrienne."

"See you in a minute."

She started tottering across the room, and I watched Nick watch her move. His face went from puzzled to curious to outright shocked. I had to suppress a laugh. I could practically see the word running across his forehead like the neon *Newsweek* ribbon in Grand Central: PREGNANTPREGNANTPREGNANTPREGNANTPREGNANT.

The box was beginning to feel very heavy. I shifted its weight a little and carried it over to the table. Then I looked around for somewhere to put it down. With the tablecloth covering whatever was under it so completely, I couldn't tell if the table would stand the weight. The floor around the desk was littered with paperback books and assorted trash. People had been dumping their champagne glasses indiscriminately. They'd also been damaging the merchandise. I kicked half angrily at the plastic and pushed the books carefully with the side of my foot. Some people are pigs. Truly.

I had gotten the box onto a more or less cleared square of floor when the woman came up to me, clutching a copy of *Blood Red Romance* she'd picked up someplace else in the store and wearing what I was sure was her very bravest smile. She was young and eager—she might even have been one of the women who had been around Tempesta when I first came in—and she couldn't decide if she was allowed to talk to me. I got the top of the book box open by tearing at it with all my might, breaking a fingernail in the process. Then I gathered a handful of books and stood up.

"Just a second," I said. "I'll be all set up in a minute."

"Oh, I'm not trying to hurry you!" she said. "I can wait!"

"Well, I won't make you wait too long."

"I bought this here, you know. I have the sales slip right in my purse."

In my opinion, given the way that party was going and all the mess-ups still unresolved in the background, I doubted if Gail Larson would have noticed a header dump full of Charlotte MacLeod novels going out the front door, but I didn't want to say so. It seemed like an incitement to crime. I got another handful of books out of the box and put those on the desk, too.

"There," I said.

"You don't know how much I admire you," the young woman said. "I read that article about you in *People*. If I ever saw a dead body, I think I'd just faint."

"Fainting might have been better than what I did do," I said.

"Oh, no. Crime is so awful these days, really. The police just can't handle it. There aren't enough of them. We *need* people like you."

A New York assistant DA named Luis Martinez had told me, on more than one occasion, that what the police really needed was for me to take a long vacation, preferably in Pago Pago. I didn't tell her that. I took her book, grabbed for the chair Gail had put out for us to sit on and sat on it. Then I started to edge it forward, keeping my knees together and my feet flat. It went slowly and it made a squeak, but at least it got me close enough to grab one of the pens.

The woman beamed at me. "I've got all your books," she said. "I've got them in hardcover. Even the first one. I didn't hear about that until it came out in paperback, but I bought it then and I liked it so much I ordered the hardcover to keep. At Waldenbooks. I probably could have come right down here and bought it without—are you all right?"

I looked down at my left foot, out of sight under the tablecloth. I had stopped moving the chair forward. Without the tablecloth, I might have been able to get my knees under the desk. With it, I was never going to fit. I'd put my foot forward to steady myself while I signed.

Now I wiggled that foot a little and bit my lip. There really isn't any other feeling like it, that feeling of stepping into flesh. I felt the sweat on my forehead and put my hand up to brush it away. I looked up and saw Adrienne coming toward me, running really, a vision in velvet and perfectly plaited braids.

"Miss McKenna?" the woman said.

*"Patience,"* Adrienne said.

"McKenna?" Nick said.

"Get her out of here," I said. "Get her out of here *now.*"

Maybe we really should be married. There are times when we have something very much like ESP. Nick grabbed Adrienne around the waist, tucked her under his arm and went plowing through the crowd in the direction of the open door.

I pushed the chair back as far as it would go and looked down again. There was nothing to see. The tablecloth hung perfectly. If I hadn't put my foot under there, I'd never have known it wasn't an empty space.

*Evelyn,* I thought.

I reached for the tablecloth and pulled it back. I stared at the navy-blue gabardine suit and the little veiled hat.

Stuck under that table, neck wrapped in a bright green paisley scarf, was the body of Mrs. Harold P. Keeley.

# EIGHT

The homicide detective they sent from wherever Baltimore keeps its homicide detectives was a woman. Her partner was not, but he didn't really count. Like most investigative teams, this one had a dominant partner and a deferential one. *She* was dominant, all newly-elected-chairman-of-the-board brisk efficiency and periodic flashes from the polished gold of flat round earrings. *He* was deferential to the point of being functionally nonexistent. I got an impression of wispy hair and a red-and-gold-striped tie, but not much else. I was not alone. Whatever chauvinistic stereotypes might have lingered in that crowd had been washed away by crisis. Ms. Detective walked in. Ms. Detective got our attention, just by being there. Ms. Detective was forever afterward the one person we looked to whenever we had a question. Especially about ourselves.

Ms. Detective's name was Barbara Defborn. I tried to keep it in mind, but that was hard to do. She didn't show up until nearly an hour into the real craziness, when the uniformed cops had been over the scene four or five times and the men from the medical examiner's office and forensics were already stowing things in little plastic bags. The store was a mess. I'd been good after I'd first discovered the body. I hadn't shouted or screamed or give in to any kind of surface panic. I'd even tried to call the police without letting anyone know I was doing it. That sort of thing never works. Once a real mess like that gets underway, news of it seems to be airborne. At least a third of the people who had been at the party when I found Mrs. Harold P. Keeley's body were gone by the time the uniformed police got to the store. Another tenth were gone by the time the plainclothes team got there, in spite of the uniformed branch's frantic attempts to keep them herded together. Efforts at imposing order were impeded by the store's size and shape and function. There'd been barely enough room for the guests when all that was going on was a party. Now one entire corner was taken up with esoteric investigative equipment and over-sized ungainly arc lamps and nervous men and women with things that had to be done *now*. The storm had gotten worse, making it impossible for even the drunkest of us to sit on the stoop for any length of time. The bartender at the Elite VIP Lounge had no inten-tion of arguing with the cops, but he had no intention of making us comfortable either. He knew trouble when he saw it. Every once in a while somebody would wander over there, down a drink in record time and come right back. He'd have to squeeze through the front door.

I've done my time in this world feeling like an arthritic sardine. I'm tall enough to be easy to crowd. I get enough exercise so that any long-term enforced immobility makes my joints ache. I decided after fifteen minutes of having my stomach attacked by restless elbows and my foot bones assailed by spike heels that I was going to have to do something about myself if I intended to get back to the hotel in one piece. What I did was climb a mantel. It was a little uncomfortable, but it had a few things to recommend it. I was effectively out of the fray. The only way anyone was going to injure me while I was up there was to do it deliberately, and in my old age I have come to feel no compunction at all about retaliating for deliberate hurt. I was also in a position to see things none of the other civilians could. I had a clear view of the signing corner and everything going on there. I had a *better* view of the body than the people standing next to it. The people standing next to it were distracted by detail and the vagaries of artificial light. From my aerial view, I got the complete picture, in all its weirdness.

Somebody had left a little tin disposable ashtray on the bookshelf closest to my left foot. I got hold of it, got my cigarettes and lit up. The medical examiner's people had the body on its back, getting it ready to be stuffed into a bag and carted out—finally. That they hadn't done it sooner might have seemed strange to me if I hadn't been involved in three other cases. In a straightforward crime—a wife standing over her dead husband with a discharged shotgun; a brother-in-law with a piece of lead pipe in his hands and a sister's husband with a gash in his head—the police like to get the body out as soon as possible. There isn't much anybody but the ME can do with it in situations like that, and nothing much the ME can do with it either. Bring it in. Poke it around. Write a report. In all likelihood, the culprit is in custody—and confessing his head off—long before that report gets written. It's different in cases where there are questions. Then the homicide detectives like to check over everything, corpse included. What had delayed the homicide detectives, I didn't know, but delayed they had been, and delayed the body had been. I didn't blame the Baltimore uniformed police at all, or the ME's people. I've seen a man dead from strangulation. Whatever had happened to Mrs. Harold P. Keeley, whatever the killer meant to suggest had happened, she hadn't died because someone put a scarf around her neck and pulled.

No bulging eyes, no lolling tongue, no blue tinge to the skin, no rigor. I tapped ash into my little tin ashtray and watched them cover her face. If she had been dead long enough—if she'd died, for instance, early in the day—none of those signs would have been present by the time we found her. I didn't think that was going to wash as an explanation. The ME's people were having a hard time moving her. That was probably rigor coming up. I did a few calculations and came to the startling conclusion that she must have been killed within an hour before the party started. It would have made even more sense if she'd been killed while the party was in progress, but I couldn't see how that could have been done. Killed and folded up and provided with somebody else's scarf—Mrs. Harold P. Keeley would never have owned any article of clothing that could be described as "bright green paisley."

One of the men who was trying to move her slipped, stubbed his toe, swore, stumbled. The edge of the bag got away from him. The nylon flap that had been covering her face dropped again. When I saw her this time, she had her head turned to the left side and her right ear exposed. I leaned forward suddenly. Along the strip of skin just underneath her ear and above her jaw was what looked like a long streak of blue eye shadow. *Bright* blue eye shadow, the kind that comes in a powder the manufacturer promises is "infused with youthful oils." I hadn't known Mrs. Harold P. Keeley long, but I'd pegged her well enough to realize she would no more have worn bright blue eye shadow than she would have owned a bright green paisley scarf.

The stumbling man got hold of himself, flipped the nylon back over her face and started to zip up. I felt something tugging on my feet and looked down. Gail Larson was there, holding a plastic champagne glass full of something much darker, and probably much stronger, than New York State champagne.

"Johnnie Walker," she said, offering the glass to me. "You want a slug?"

"That's okay," I said.

"What happened to that nice little girl? I thought she belonged to you."

"Adrienne's back at the hotel. I explained the situation to that man over there"—I pointed to one of the uniformed cops who had been first on the scene—"and he let Nick and Phoebe bring her back."

"Phoebe pregnant?"

"Very. And I didn't want Adrienne in the middle of all this."

"I don't blame you."

She looked back over the crowd. The fan I'd been talking to when I'd found the body was being interviewed by the nondescript partner. Ms. Barbara Defborn had started in on Christopher Brand. The romance writers, including Tempesta Stewart, were all huddled into a clot near the front door. I sighed. Once we got out of here, all hell was going to break loose for real. Tempesta and Amelia both had that *look* on their faces: the one they got before they decided to make serious trouble.

Gail was more interested in Christopher, doing his best to look belligerent and sexy in response to Defborn's almost schoolteacherly calmness. He wasn't getting anywhere. The great thatch of shaggy gray hair, the truck driver's shoulders and slender, almost feminine waist—none of it was doing any good. Ms. Defborn didn't look within a hundred years of losing her patience, never mind falling for him.

Gail jabbed her plastic glass in the air. "You know what he told me? That Christopher Brand? He said this would be *good for the store.*"

"Are you serious?"

"Of course I'm serious. We got stuck together when the cops first came in. I couldn't get away from him. And he kept telling me and telling me not to worry, I'd make a mint after this, all Baltimore would be trooping through here in a few days. It was insane."

"I wonder if he's telling Ms. Defborn about the fight he had with Keeley back at the Inner Harbor."

"If he isn't, he ought to be," Gail said. "You know how Tempesta is. She saw the whole thing. She'll never keep her mouth shut."

"Do you suppose there is something irregular about his divorce from Haverman? Could she have been right?"

"I don't know," Gail said. "Mrs. Keeley was a very strange person when it came to gossip. Some kinds she was really good at. *Real* scandal. You know, somebody embezzling money or somebody dealing drugs or somebody who'd been in a mental institution and wasn't telling anybody. With that sort of thing, she was practically clairvoyant. But with men-and-women stuff . . . it's hard to explain. She didn't like men much. When sex-related things happened, she tended to believe the women. A few years ago, there was this girl, married to an old man with a lot of money. It turned out later she'd been feeding him arsenic and sleeping with his sons the whole time. Our Mrs. Keeley believes to this day—and the truth was on the front page of the *Sun,* for God's sake—that *he* was the one to blame and *she* was the saint."

"What's *Mr.* Harold P. Keeley like?"

"Dead."

Across the room, Ms. Defborn dismissed Christopher Brand and motioned to Tempesta Stewart. Tempesta went trotting over, her hips twitching, her face frozen into smug malice. Christopher gave her a look. Then he stalked off.

"What I don't understand," I said, "is how she was gotten in here. I was watching the body while they were bagging it up. She couldn't have died more than an hour before the party started. With the store open and all—"

"The store wasn't open," Gail said.

"It wasn't?"

"It usually is on Tuesdays," she said, "but I just couldn't handle it today. I opened from eleven to two, and then I locked up again and did some errands. I didn't think there was going to be any problem. With things here, I mean. There were *other* problems. I waited and waited for the champagne. It was supposed to arrive at noon. Nothing. I called the supplier and got the most God-awful gibberish—"

"What kind of gibberish?"

"It's on the way. The truck has had a breakdown. It'll be there in time. Don't worry. The usual crap. Then I got through to somebody who sounded as officious as hell and *she* told me *I'd* told her I was going to pick the stuff up myself, and it was ready anytime I wanted it.

I was about ready to kick somebody. So I closed the store down and went to get the stuff. But I wouldn't jump to conclusions if I were you. I would have closed the store down anyway. I had to get the plastic glasses and the cigarettes and some extra pens. Writers are always complaining about how there aren't any pens at signings."

"Well, at least we don't have to look for a ghost. Somebody just brought her in here while you were out and shoved her under the table. Was that tablecloth thing all set up at the time?"

"Oh, yeah," Gail said. "Actually, everything Mrs. Keeley promised to do was done. The table was set up. The posters were set up. The displays were moved around. The displays I usually use were stuck in the back room, not that there's any *room* for them there—"

"Wait," I said. "Mrs. Keeley was supposed to do all that?"

"Mrs. Keeley was supposed to do all that and Evelyn was supposed to get the boxes of books unpacked and the money set up. That was part of the deal. I mean, after all, this is *not* a general bookstore. And you know I love having *you,* and I wouldn't have minded having Phoebe either if she were promoting those Sarah English romantic suspense things you two are involved in." Sarah English had been Adrienne's mother. *"But,"* Gail went on, "this is a small business *and* I can't afford to hire a lot of extra help just to put on a party for charity. *So* Evelyn worked it all out, and got Mrs. Harold P. and her organization to do the social part—actually I put Evelyn in touch with the Baltimore Book Lovers Association and then—"

"Wait," I said, "I don't understand—"

"Oh, I don't either," Gail said. "I haven't understood anything for weeks. Evelyn is a very nice woman," Gail faltered. "At least—"

"I'm wondering where she is, too," I said.

"Do you figure she killed Mrs. Keeley and took off? Why would she?"

"I don't know," I said. "But she surely is missing. Jon's got every reason to be worried. She was never a great publicist, but at least she attended her own tours. And you know how she is about charities."

"Everybody knows how Evelyn is about charities. Although what makes her decide if something is a charity, I'll never figure out. Right-wing stuff. Left-wing stuff. The Women's Reproductive Rights Defense Fund and the National Coalition for the Rights of the Unborn. You know she collected for both of those?"

"I've stopped paying attention to what she collects for," I said. "It gives me a headache. All her organizations have titles that sound like bad jokes."

"I wonder where she is."

I shrugged. The bad with Mrs. Harold P. Keeley's body in it was going out the door. I was going to be glad to get rid of it. Tempesta Stewart was stalking away from Ms. Barbara Defborn. I wished Phoebe with me, impossible though that was. Phoebe always has a salutary effect on my incipient depressions.

"Gail," I said, "did your Mrs. Harold P. Keeley wear eye shadow?"

"Eye shadow? You must be joking. She wore a lot of lipstick. Brown-red lipstick. You saw her."

"I saw her."

"Eye shadow would have been like ruffles. She really hated ruffles."

"What else did she really hate?"

Gail didn't even think about it. "Practically everything," she said.

From the other side of the room, Barbara Defborn called out in a voice so clipped and pronounced, it must have been subjected to years of diction lessons.

"Ms. McKenna? I'll take you now."

# NINE

I have been through dozens of police interviews. Sometimes, at the very start of a mess, I think I've been through hundreds. I walked over to where Barbara Defborn was standing, near a little display of Robert B. Parker paperbacks, expecting the kind of routine I'm usually put through when I have to talk to police officers who don't know me. Getting a reputation as an amateur detective doesn't usually do wonderful things for your relationships with professional law enforcement personnel. I thought this session was going to be worse than most. People who live outside New York can be very strange about people who live in it. A lot of them are convinced that New Yorkers think they're better than everyone else, and smarter than everyone else, and tougher than everyone else. This is especially true of the people who work for the police, fire and social services departments of what they themselves think of as "provincial cities." I hadn't found the least thing "provincial" about Baltimore, but I was sure Barbara Defborn would think I had.

I got a surprise. When I came up to her, she put out her hand, shook mine and smiled. She wasn't just cordial, she was friendly. She was also younger than I'd thought she was when looking at her from a distance. Her severe black suit and starched white blouse gave off an air of maturity that would have been better suited to a much older woman. She might have been all of five years older than I was, but she couldn't have been more than that. Her face was relatively unlined. Her hair was only lightly flecked with gray, and obviously neither dyed nor frosted. She'd had sense enough not to add one of those abominable little bow ties to her very elegant suit.

She glanced around the room, seeming amused. "Real mess in here, isn't it?" she said. "Wouldn't you rather go outside?"

"I'll go if you want to," I said, "but it's cold out there."

"And wet," she agreed. "On the other hand, I've got Officer Bradbury stationed at the Elite, and at least we'd be able to talk there without being overheard. I've been getting the definite impression that those people"—she nodded toward the romance writers—"eavesdrop as a matter of principle."

"Actually, it's not just those people," I said. "You'd have to say the same thing about Christopher Brand."

"And probably Mr. Lowry and maybe Gail Larson, and certainly half the rest of the people here. Sometimes I think human nature is a terrible thing, especially the natures of humans who are *not* what my partner would call scum. You know what most of these people are going to do? They're going to go home and be upset. They're going to have a hard time sleeping for a couple of days. Then the fear is going to wear off, and they're going to *love* it."

"Guilty," I said.

"At least you're not *just* a voyeur. And a mutual friend of ours told me that no matter what else you were, you were definitely somebody who did not go home and start making things up just to make yourself look important. Or for any other reason. He said you had a very good grasp of the nature of facts."

"Lu Martinez," I said. "How do you know Lu Martinez?"

"I've met him at a few law enforcement conventions. He gives good bar. He also happens to give good lectures, so whenever he's speaking I go. He gave one about you."

I winced. "Did he call me a flake?"

"In the lecture, no," Barbara Defborn said. "Later, in the bar, he did say something about your being 'one of those women who make you think Gracie Allen wasn't joking.' Shall we go?"

"Do I get to drink?"

"You do and I don't."

"I'll get my coat."

We got a few strange looks when we walked out, but I was beyond caring—even though I knew Amelia would come knocking on my door at whatever hour of the morning she got back to the hotel, demanding an explanation. We went out into the storm and fought our way against the wind in the direction of the Elite VIP Lounge. There was a lot of traffic on the street, enough to make me realize it wasn't as late as I'd thought it had been. Nine o'clock or nine-thirty, I thought.

Maybe ten. I clutched at the collar of my coat, bringing it up over the back of my long fall of blond hair. Barbara Defborn didn't bother trying to protect her own. The weather was an outrage. The snow had turned to freezing rain. The sidewalk was a solid sheet of ice. She slipped and slid along the pavement, bringing all her concentration to bear on staying upright.

In the Elite, she waved at the uniformed man sitting over a cup of coffee at the bar—Officer Bradbury, obviously—and then took me to a table against the wall. The table was as far away from everyone and everything as we could get in that place. The Universal Law of the Relationship of Weather and Alcohol Consumption operated in Baltimore just the way it did in New York. It was a Tuesday night. If the Elite was like most bars, and I had no reason to think it wasn't, Tuesdays were probably not a regularly busy time. This Tuesday, the place was packed, and not with a spillover from the TBDI debacle either. I could pick out the three or four people who had been at the party. They were just a little too well dressed. The rest of the crowd weren't seedy, but they were comfortable. They all seemed to be in jeans and sweaters, the after-work uniform of the American middle class.

Barbara Defborn signaled to the waiter, who must have known who she was. He came right over. She pointed to me and said, "I think Ms. McKenna's usual is Drambuie on the rocks. You can get me a cup of coffee."

The waiter nodded and hurried away. I got out my cigarettes.

"That must have been some lecture Lu gave," I said. "Or was that in the bar, too?"

"No, that was in the lecture," Barbara Defborn said. "He said you drank Drambuie when you were seriously drinking and Baileys Original Irish when you wanted to relax. He said you were anorexic."

"I'm not, really. I just forget to eat."

"You look anorexic," Barbara Defborn said. "On the other hand, you don't look *dangerously* anorexic. You want to know what we're doing here?"

"Give it a second. You must be a celebrity around this place. The waiter's coming back."

The waiter was indeed coming back. He had Drambuie. He had coffee. He put both, and a little pitcher of milk or cream, down on the table. Then he hurried away. I looked at the tables around us, found one other person who was having coffee and determined that that person was drinking it black. That was too bad. I wanted to know if everybody got little pitchers of milk or cream, or if noncelebrities got stuck with those little plastic tubs of nondairy creamer.

I took a sip of my drink—iced, but not watered. I lit my cigarette.

"If you want me to interfere," I said, "you didn't have to ask. I can't help myself."

"I don't think interfering is how I'd put it," Barbara Defborn said. "There are aspects of this mess— How do you think Margaret Keeley died?"

"I don't know," I said. "I know how I don't think she died. I don't think she was strangled."

"Very good." Barbara nodded. "She certainly wasn't strangled. Oh, I suppose I could be wrong. The coroner's report could come back and surprise us all. But I don't think it will."

"I don't either. She didn't—look right for being strangled."

"Very good," Barbara said. "I'll tell you something else. Something you probably couldn't see for yourself. When I looked over the body I found, on the back of her neck, a puncture wound about the size of a—"

"Oh Jesus," I said.

"Nasty," Barbara agreed. "More than nasty, really, because it suggests a sequence of events I don't like at all. In the first place, most people don't carry around the kind of implement that could produce that sort of wound. A knitting needle wouldn't work unless it was tempered steel, but even that would have caused a lot of muck and mess. This was a very clean wound. I can think of maybe half a dozen items that might have done the job. One of those fine-work awls antique restorers use for close work on wood. Or one of those immense surgical extraction needles made to draw major amounts of pus out of infected wounds. Nothing any of those people back there"—she made a gesture in the general direction of The Butler Did It—"would just accidentally have hanging around in a back pocket or the bottom of a purse."

"Premeditation," I said.

"At the very least. The *other* thing has to do with how the wound got there. How it *didn't* get there was by someone walking up to Mrs. Keeley from behind while she was dusting the bookshelves. She had to have been unconscious when it happened. If she hadn't been, there would *really* have been a mess."

"Conked?" I suggested.

"I'm inclined to say drugged. I didn't see any bruising around the head. Of course, it's like all the rest of this. I might be wrong."

"Why do I have the distinct feeling I'd rather be in Philadelphia?"

"Wait," she said. "It gets worse. What do you know about Margaret Johnson Keeley?"

"Not much," I admitted. "She wasn't a personality type I was inclined to like. Hostile. Nosy. Self-righteous. I think Gail Larson said something about her husband being dead. I don't know if that's true or not."

"Her husband is most definitely dead," Barbara said. "Died about five years ago. Her daughter's in the Peace Corps in Asia somewhere. I don't think they've spoken in years. I know all this already because around the time she was widowed, she got very involved in local good works. The Baltimore Book Lovers Association you know about. She also ran a Support Your Local Police group for a couple of years. The thing is, what can't have happened here is a family killing. There was no family around to commit it. Which means—"

"Somebody at the party," I said.

"Or somebody connected to the store. Or somebody—I don't know. But whatever the motive was, it wasn't the usual sort of thing. Her wallet's missing, but her money isn't—"

"What?"

"She kept her money in a separate billfold-purse thing—"

"The kind of thing Coach sells," I said. "I know what you mean."

"It wasn't from Coach. Mrs. Keeley didn't have that kind of money. And I shouldn't say the wallet's missing. We'll probably find it at her house. All she kept in it were pictures and minor documents. The certificate she received from her school for being voted Teacher of the Year. That kind of thing. She had stuff like that going way back. That wallet was ancient and it was *crammed.*"

"You think somebody may have wanted something that was in there?"

"I can't see why." She looked into her coffee, which was still undoctored by milk and getting cold. She took a sip of it and made a face. "I hate coffee," she said. "I wish I could find something else to drink.

Soft drinks are fattening. Diet soft drinks taste terrible. Perrier is too yuppie . . ."

"Club soda has too much salt," I recited.

Barbara said, "Mmm." Then she poured milk into her coffee until the concoction was nearly bone white and took a great gulp. "This Evelyn Kleig who's missing," she said. "What do you know about *her?*"

I laughed. "You got a couple of hours?"

"You could stick to pertinent details," Barbara said.

"Well," I started. Then I stopped. There was music playing in the background, but nothing I recognized. I let it slide over me. "You know," I said, "the odd thing is, pertinent details may be the one thing I don't have about Evelyn. A couple of hours ago, I thought I did, but then I had this talk with Jon Lowry—"

"Our reclusive billionaire," Barbara said faintly.

"He is a nerd, isn't he? He's a nice nerd, though. Anyway, I was talking to him about something else—this was at the hotel, before the party—and he said something about Evelyn having come from Baltimore. I'd always thought she was a native New Yorker. Do you think that has something to do with it? If Evelyn *was* from Baltimore, she might have known Mrs. Keeley when she was a child—"

"Nope. Margaret Keeley wasn't from Baltimore. She and her husband came here about two years before the husband died. He worked for some big chemical company somewhere. I think he was transferred."

"From where?"

"Cleveland?" Barbara said. "Maybe it was Akron. Somewhere in Ohio."

"I know why I thought Evelyn was from New York," I said. "She graduated from Hunter. Practically everybody who goes to Hunter is from the city, or close. It's that kind of a place."

"Well, you may have been right. Maybe Jon Lowry is the one who's confused."

"Oh, Jon's confused all right," I said, "but I'd be surprised if he were confused about Evelyn. He dotes on Evelyn."

"What about the rest of them?"

"You mean the tour?"

"Yes."

I lit another cigarette and shrugged. "I suppose most of us were terminally exasperated with her. She was a flake in a lot of ways. She didn't listen to people. On the other hand . . . well, you take Christopher Brand."

"*You* take Christopher Brand. He tried to put a hand up my skirt."

"He always does," I said. "Anyway, the thing is, he's awful on tour. So awful, people refuse to work with him. That's what Evelyn told me, and Gail Larson told me the same thing later. Apparently, most bookstores won't have him in to sign. The man's got a whole army of ex-wives. That's an expensive proposition even with the prenuptial agreements he's always made them swallow. Anyway, if a writer's popular enough, or famous enough—and Christopher is both—signings can really up the sales of books. And he needs to sell every book. He must have been hurting bad with none of the stores willing to have him. Evelyn put him on this tour and strong-armed half the mystery bookstore owners in the United States into putting up with his act."

"So he's exasperated but he needs her."

"Tempesta Stewart, too," I said. "The woman's some kind of terrorist—"

"We know all about Miss Tempesta Stewart in Baltimore," Barbara said. "She's been in before. At some kind of vigilante rally."

"Actually," I said, "I don't think most of us paid much attention to Evelyn. She was PR. Basically, writers notice PR when something goes wrong with the publicity. Not before."

"And nothing has?"

"The trip has been a dream," I conceded. "Exhausting. Overscheduled from the word go. But still a dream. You don't *know* how wonderful it is to arrive at bookstore after bookstore and always have books to sign."

"You've gone to sign books at a bookstore and not had any books to sign?"

"More times than I can count."

"Well, I guess that takes care of everything," Barbara said. "Everything for now. All I want you to do is tell me anything you might find out, accidentally or otherwise. The Baltimore end of this, I'm not worried about. I've been around a long time. But those people— Who is that immense woman with the beaded dress?"

"Amelia Samson."

"Amelia Samson who was on *60 Minutes?* Who's got a castle somewhere?"

"Rhinebeck, New York. I've been there. It's quite a place."

"I'm sure it is. Talk to these people, will you, please? In all likelihood, we'll catch up to your Ms. Kleig somewhere and that will be that, but you never know. I don't know the types well enough to feel entirely secure about the conclusions I'm coming to. And if you help out, I can always tell Lu at the next convention that I know all about you. You want another drink?"

"I think I'd rather get back and see how Adrienne is doing."

"Good idea. Tell Miss Damereaux and Mr. Carras I'll talk to them in the morning."

"We're not suspects?"

"Well," Barbara said, "as far as I can tell, Mr. Carras was with an eight-year-old child all afternoon and Miss Damereaux couldn't have stopped throwing up long enough to kill anybody. As for you—"

"Yes?"

"Lu says it always surprises him you eat meat."

# TEN

I should have expected Adrienne to be waiting up for me when I got back to the hotel. Even with nothing in particular going on, she tends to keep watch until she knows I'm safely home and in bed. I knew for a fact that while I'd been on this tour, she'd never gone to sleep until after my nightly call. It was as if she needed to continually anchor me, to prove to herself that I was solid. I wished I knew whether she had always been like that, or had only become like that after her mother was killed. I didn't pretend to understand what effect the murder of a parent would have on a child. Most of the time, she seemed stable, intelligent, good-humored and *normal*. That was all I asked. When the nightmares came along—and they still did, although less frequently than they had the year before—I took care of them the best I could.

She was sticking her head out the door of a room halfway down the hall when I got off the elevator, not the door to the room I thought of as "mine." She saw me right away, and started gesturing frantically. Behind her, the room she was leaning out of was in darkness. Her hair was unbraided and pulled back off her forehead with a rubber band. I guessed that when I got to her I'd find her in one of the elaborately embroidered nightgowns she loved so much. I have a lot of deeply held convictions, inherited from my mother, about the kind of money that should and should not be spent on children. Ninety-dollar night-gowns are obviously an extravagance that properly belongs to adults. I bought them for her anyway. If I hadn't, Phoebe would have.

She slipped into the hall and I approached her, shutting the door behind her with an almost undetectable *click.*

*"Shh,"* she said. "Phoebe's sleeping. She's going to have a baby and she needs a lot of rest."

"Who told you Phoebe was going to have a baby?" I kissed her on the cheek.

"Anybody can tell Phoebe is going to have a baby," she said. "She throws up all the time. And I mean *all the time.* I thought morning sickness was supposed to happen in the morning."

Since Adrienne and I have conversations like this constantly—God only knows where she and Courtney pick up these things—I decided to let the exploration of just where she'd picked up her information about morning sickness slide. Adrienne and Courtney are not your ordinary eight-year-olds. If they want to know about something, they don't dither around resenting the fact that there's no information in the latest issue of *Sesame Street Magazine.* They go down to the Forty-second Street branch of the New York Public Library and look it up. They have a facility with card catalogues that would turn a DLS green.

"Morning sickness can happen any time," I told her, figuring information was better than misinformation, and she knew half this stuff already. I sat down on the floor with my back against the wall. My back ached. "How are you?"

"I'm okay, I guess. I think it's a good idea for Phoebe to have a baby. Phoebe is the kind of person who *ought* to have a baby."

"I'm with you," I said.

"The only thing that worries me is, I think Phoebe's baby is going to have the *entire contents* of F. A. O. Schwarz by the time it's two months old."

"Why not?" I said. *"You* have the entire contents of F. A. O. Schwarz, *and* a personal computer, *and* a closet full of designer sneakers, *and* a new dress. I liked the dress."

She eyed me warily. "You going to yell at me about that?"

"I'm not even going to tell Nick just how much more expensive it was than all your other party dresses."

She blew a stream of breath into her bangs. "Thanks," she said.

"No problem," I said.

"I'm sleeping in here with Phoebe," she said. "Nick's down in your room. Phoebe's clothes are all down there, too. Nick offered to move them, but Phoebe was too sick to supervise."

"That's okay. We'll get to those tomorrow. Don't you think you ought to be asleep?"

"Maybe," she said. She looked toward the floor, at her long toes peeking out from under her nightgown. I knew the signs. Adrienne always gets like that when she wants to ask a Really Serious Question.

For Adrienne, all Really Serious Questions concern the life and death of Sarah Caulfield English, her mother.

"Patience," she said. "That woman who died, tonight at that store, did she—I mean, was it the same way as my mama?"

"That depends on what you mean," I said.

"I *know* she was murdered," Adrienne said. "That's all over the hotel. I mean, was it—the same *thing?*"

"I don't think so," I said. "The coroner—do you remember about the coroner?" She nodded. "The coroner has to do tests," I said, "and then we'll know for sure. But people often look different ways when they die different ways. Sarah—your mother— What am I trying to say?"

"She looked different when she died."

"Yes, she did."

"Did you see Mrs. Baumgarten from upstairs from us when *she* died?"

"Mrs. Baumgarten? Why do you want to know about Mrs. Baumgarten?"

"Because she died the way she was supposed to," Adrienne said. "She was old and she went to sleep and she never woke up again. And I was wondering what *that* looked like. People hardly ever seem to die the way they're supposed to. It ought to be the easiest thing in the world, but it just doesn't happen. People always seem to be—to be—"

"Killing other people?" I said.

"It's not just this woman in the bookstore," Adrienne said defensively. "And I *know* Reverend Patcher is full of it with all that about our universal responsibility for violence or whatever—I talked it over with Courtney and we looked it up in Aristotle and we know it doesn't make any sense—"

"You've been reading *Aristotle?*"

"I don't think we understood it all," Adrienne said.

"Right," I said.

"But the thing is," Adrienne said. Then she sighed. "I'm not making any sense, am I?"

"You're making perfect sense," I told her. "I just don't have the answers you need. I'm not God, Adrienne. I'm not even Aristotle."

"Well, if God does have the answers I need, He's going to spend a lot of time talking when I finally get to heaven." She turned around and looked at her door. "I guess I'd better go to bed. I did promise Nick I'd go right to sleep. And he was really good about the dress."

"Want me to tuck you in?"

She shook her head. "Just about anything wakes Phoebe up," she said. "And I mean *anything*. And as soon as she wakes up, she starts getting sick again."

"Know where I am?"

"Yeah. I'll come knock if I need you. Night."

"I love you," I said.

She put her arms around my neck and kissed me, hard. Then she grabbed for the knob and disappeared through the door.

I sat there for a few minutes, watching the blank slab of wood. I don't remember what my life was like before I had Adrienne for company. I often wonder if I'm any good for her. What I know about children, beyond the fact that they probably shouldn't have couture Dior until they reach the age of eighteen, wouldn't fill the back of a business card.

I sat in the hall much longer than I'd intended to. I was in one of those states of waking coma we used to call "veging out," and when I finally did make myself get up and get moving again, I was completely out of it. It had been a long day. The two days coming up looked to be longer still. I wandered in the direction of my room thinking about the most trivial things, like where Nick was keeping his socks. Back in New York, he keeps them in my refrigerator. He says he likes the coolness on his feet when he first gets dressed in the morning. Since the hotel room had no refrigerator, I had to assume he was going to do without the coolness or risk getting them wet by hanging them out the window in a little plastic bag.

I found my key, let myself into the room and walked to the end of the entrance foyer to find Nick lying on his stomach on the bed that had been Phoebe's, Walkman earphones over his head and a lot of legal-sized paper spread out over the pillow. He held up a finger to tell me it would only be a minute—Nick is *always* working on *something*—and I walked over and took the earphones off his head. Chuck Berry, doing "No Particular Place to Go." I threw the earphones on his ass.

"Talk to me," I said. "It's been a long day."

He turned over on his back and put his hands behind his head.

Adrienne says he looks like Christopher Reeve, and that's true—although he's both taller and heavier—but there's something about him that lets you know he could never be an actor. Everything in Nick is linear, solid, logical. He once told me there were only two ways anyone ever worked their way out of poverty: crime, or a commitment to rationality so profound that the mere possibility of the existence of anything else dropped right out of your head. Nick did not play the lottery, bet on Rangers games or watch the sort of television game show where winning was determined by tosses of the dice or spins of the wheel. He had erased the word "luck" from his vocabulary. There was only work. The results of work were invariable. Do it hard enough, long enough, and you got where you were going.

Since Nick had obviously got where he was going—I'd only recently convinced him to buy a decent suit, but his lack of one hadn't been the result of an inability to afford one; he just hates buying clothes—I left all discussion of the true nature of the universe at the door of whatever room I met him in. Besides, his outlook was a comfort to me. My world often seems to be made up of nothing *but* luck.

I shoved him over on the bed and sat down beside him. "I was just talking to Adrienne. She's taking this better than I thought she would."

"She's a solid kid," Nick agreed. "Do you want to strangle David first, or are you going to let me do it?"

"Oh well."

"There's no 'oh well' about it. I told him when he first started hitting on Phoebe— Of course, we'd have to find him first, there's that. At the moment, I'd most dearly love to find him."

I shrugged off my coat, tossed it in the direction of the vanity table, and missed. I thought about going over to pick it up and decided not to. Then I leaned down and started getting out of my shoes.

"What did you mean, he disappeared?" I said.

"I came in this morning, I found a note on my desk. 'Sorry about the inconvenience. I'm going out of town. Maybe I won't be back.' He had a full client schedule today, too, and I was coming down here. Janet just about freaked. I went into his office and found his desk half cleaned out. His pictures of Phoebe were gone. His case files and stuff were still there."

"Did you call his apartment?"

"Three times, once from Philadelphia. I even talked to his super. He left last night around eleven. One overnight bag. Didn't tell anybody he was going. The super knew because David knocked on his door and asked to have his mail picked up. For about a month."

"It's got to have something to do with Phoebe," I said. "It doesn't make sense otherwise."

"I'm sure it's got something to do with Phoebe," Nick said. "What, I don't know. Where, I don't know either. At the moment, I don't know how much I care. I'd like to break the little bastard's neck."

"Maybe he was on his way here."

"If he was, he'd already be here. And we'd have heard from him by now."

"All right." I stood up and pulled my sweater over my head. "This day just keeps getting worse and worse," I said. "I had a talk with that police detective, Barbara Defborn." I told him what she'd said about the weapon, or instrument, or whatever I was supposed to call it. "And if that isn't bad enough," I finished, "Evelyn's missing. Which makes it look awful for Evelyn. I like Evelyn. Or at least I don't dislike her. Anyway, I'd rather have it work out some way that makes *emotional* sense for once."

"You mean, so the murderer is someone you hate?"

"How about Christopher Brand?" I asked him. "I could see him locked up without a moment of regret."

"You and half a million other people. Why would Christopher Brand kill the president of the Baltimore Book Lovers Association?"

I had just let my skirt fall to my ankles. I started bending over to pick it up, and stopped. The odd thing was, I had an answer for that one, or the beginnings of an answer. Why it hadn't occurred to me back at the store, I'd never know.

"Jenna Lee Haverman," I said. "When I was talking to Gail Larson, I remembered Christopher and Mrs. Keeley fighting, but I didn't remember what they'd been fighting about. Now I do. They were fighting about one of his ex-wives. Mrs. Keeley was saying she knew he'd tricked this ex-wife out of the settlement he owed her, and she could — No, she didn't say she could. She said any good lawyer could prove it. Well, maybe any good lawyer could. Maybe she knew something that could get that decision reversed. Everybody knows how hard up

Chris is for money. He spends it like crazy and the ex-wives bleed him even with the prenuptial agreements. If Mrs. Keeley had a way—"

"Patience," Nick said.

"It's not that bad a theory," I insisted.

Nick sat up. *"Braverman v. Brand,* Superior Court of the State of New York, January 1972."

"You know the reference?"

"I ought to. That's one of the most famous cases in New York State divorce law. You can't pass the bar without answering three questions about it. Believe me, that thing is airtight. It established a precedent that's been used ever since. *And* it took nearly three years to tie up, with both sides hiring private detectives right and left. There's nothing about either of them, or their relationship, or that agreement, left to find. You look at the file sometime. They've got everything in there but each other's blood types."

"Are you sure?"

"Absolutely positive. Of course, David's our expert on divorce, and under the circumstances—"

"Do you think he'll ever come back and do the right thing by Phoebe?"

"I think the only right thing he could do by Phoebe now is to leave her the hell alone. Come to bed, McKenna. It's late and I'm tired."

"I want to take a shower."

Nick retrieved the earphones and put them back on his head.

I went down the hall to the bathroom, turned on the light and shut myself inside. I turned on the water and adjusted the shower nozzle until I had a hard, driving spray. Then I got out of the rest of my clothes and leaned up to the mirror to check for wrinkles.

If I'd found any wrinkles, I might not have found the other thing. I am firmly convinced that the first time I see a line on my face, I am going to descend into a neurotic spasm. My genetics were holding out. My mother hadn't had a wrinkle until she was sixty. My body seemed to be taking its cue from her.

It was while I was pulling back the shower curtain to step into the bathtub that I saw it, and the fact that I saw it at all was one of those accidents Nick spends so much of his time pretending don't exist. A trick of the light. An awkward move in the wrong direction. I saw the flash of matte blue and pulled my hands back before they were touched by water.

It was right there in the creases between the ends of my fingers and my palms, on both hands, a thick powdered line of blue turning to paste from my sweat. I touched the tip of one of my fingers to the line on the opposite hand. The blue smeared. I thought of the line of blue above Margaret Keeley's jaw. When I turned my hands so that the light shone directly on the line, it looked bright, too.

It felt gritty.

# ELEVEN

"Listen," the voice on the phone said the next morning, "I don't know what you're up to, but I'm *not* going to fall for it. I'm *not.*"

I raised my head off the flat of the bed—for some reason, although I go to sleep with a million pillows under me, they're always on the floor by the time I wake up—and caught Nick, already awake and dressed, working through papers on the other side of the room. I wondered vaguely if they were the same papers he'd been working on the night before. I wondered what time it was. One of Nick's peculiarities is that, barring forcible wakening by a determined outside agent, he *always* sleeps for exactly eight hours straight. Since he'd dropped off just about eleven, it had to be after seven. Since no matter what time it was, I was going to think it was too early, I decided not to bother with something that was only going to start an argument.

With somebody.

I propped myself up on my elbows and looked around. My cigarettes were in plain sight, but Nick hated it when I smoked first thing in the morning. In fact, Nick hated it when I smoked. So did Phoebe. So did Adrienne. I turned my head and saw that Nick had pulled the curtains, opening the room to the day. The day didn't have much I'd want to be open to. Black clouds. Gray air. Wind. Little dots of something that might have been snow. One of the things Evelyn had been careful to do for this tour was to keep a supply of guidebooks and Chamber of Commerce handbooks ready, just in case any of us wanted to be sensible enough to read them. It was a good idea. Local media love it when New York Writers (note capitals) can enthuse knowledgeably about the surrounding territory. A serious newspaper like the Baltimore *Sun* tended to be above that sort of thing, but smaller papers in smaller towns had been known to run very good reviews of a visiting writer's book just because the visiting writer had been able to call the mayor's husband by his first name and spell

Chicadiggawa Pond without a hitch. Phoebe always checked those guidebooks. I never did, except to look at the weather charts. The weather charts for Baltimore had been heartening. Almost always mild. Almost always sunny. What was this?

"Patience?" the voice on the phone said.

I rolled over and got my cigarettes off the night table. Phoebe calls me Patience. Nick and Adrienne sometimes call me Patience, but rarely. My mother calls me Patience when I absolutely refuse to come wide awake at three o'clock in the morning to discuss centerpieces for the wedding. Most of my friends call me Pay or McKenna.

Nick looked up from his papers. "Is there actually anybody on the other end of that line?"

"Yes," I said. "I—"

"You *are* there," the voice said. "Good. I was beginning to think I'd called one of those heavy breathers."

The slur in the words and the logical reversal came together, and I made the connection. "Tempesta," I said. "What in the name of God—"

"It's almost eleven o'clock, Patience. If I woke you up, I don't want to hear about it. And don't take the name of the Lord in vain."

"Just a minute," I said. I put my hand over the mouthpiece and waved to Nick. "Is there coffee around here anywhere? Where are Phoebe and Adrienne?"

"Phoebe and Adrienne went to see some museum," Nick said. "We had breakfast together downstairs. Apparently, when Phoebe isn't being sick, she's eating. A lot."

"What's a lot?"

"Three orders of pancakes, two orders of hash browns, four orders of toast and grits. She ordered sausage once, but she couldn't get it down. Who's on the phone?"

"Tempesta Stewart," I said. He raised his eyebrows halfway up his forehead, but I didn't elaborate. "Coffee?"

"You can call room service when you get off the phone."

I took my hand off the mouthpiece and lit a cigarette. "Tempesta? Okay, I'm here, I'm awake and I've been too washed out to do anything to anybody. What are you talking about?"

"Were you asleep?" Tempesta said.

"I was asleep," I said.

"All morning? You haven't been downstairs once today?"

"Tempesta, for—"

*"Don't* say it. Oh Lord. You know, I was really hoping it was you. I really was. It didn't seem too likely, but the only person who did seem likely was Christopher Brand and the last person I'd want to talk to is —oh Lord, that *man."*

"Tempesta, isn't saying 'Lord' just as bad as—"

"Don't start. Just don't start. Can you get down here right away?"

"I can get down there when I've had a shower and some coffee."

"I'll come to you."

There was a click on the line, and then a dial tone. I stared at the receiver for a minute and then chucked it back into the cradle. Nick folded his hands over his papers and waited expectantly. Before I met him, I used to make lists of all the things I wanted in a man, the kind of lists some women turn into advertisements in the personals columns of highbrow magazines. It would have had to be a highbrow magazine, because at that time in my life I was convinced that intelligence was the key to everything. Maybe that was because, at the time, I was choosing my dates more for their physical perfection than for anything else. There is a cliché that says beautiful women are almost always stupid, but believe me, the stupidity of beautiful women cannot begin to sink to the depths of the stupidity of beautiful men. Now I had Nick, who was not only beautiful and intelligent, but six or seven other things I'd said I'd wanted before I was thirty. The perversity of life was holding fast. There were a lot of things I loved about Nick, but the things I'd said I'd wanted weren't among them.

One of the things I'd said I'd wanted was patience. Nick was sitting over his papers, being very patient. I swung my legs over the side of the bed and decided to take my shower before I murdered him for his patience.

"Look," I said, "I don't know what she wanted. Except I think it has nothing to do with me, but she's coming over anyway. You've met Tempesta."

"I represented her once," he said.

"You did?"

"It was a weird case. Of course, it's a matter of public record now, but I couldn't tell you anything about it then because of confidentiality. But I wanted to. Oh boy, did I want to."

"What did she do?"

"That's just it," Nick said. "She didn't. What she was accused of doing was nailing shut a door of the Downtown Church of Wicca and painting a big gold cross on the front of it."

"What's Wicca?"

"The trendy name for witchcraft. According to the people at the Downtown, etc., it's a revival of the ancient term, but I couldn't tell you about that. I've got my doubts about all these revivals of ancient terms anyway. However, she was accused of doing it and I—"

"You got her off?"

"Oh, I got her off, all right. I just wasn't supposed to."

"What?"

He shrugged. "She didn't want to be off. That's the truth. She kept running around saying, 'I am proud to take complete responsibility for this military act in the defense of God our Father,' or something like that. You know how she talks. But she literally couldn't have done it. It was a physical impossibility. You know what she is. Tallish but on the frail side. The last time she saw any serious exercise she was in sixth-grade gym class. These nails were the industrial kind, really *thick,* and they'd been pounded right through great slabs of hardwood. I might have done it, working hard. Amelia might have done it, working hard. Tempesta Stewart?"

"So what happened?"

"She got off because there was no way she couldn't," Nick said, "and now she pretends she didn't. I caught her on some CBN talk show one night when I couldn't sleep and I was flipping through the channels. She was telling everybody on earth how she'd nailed shut that door."

"Huh," I said.

"I'll go further. I don't think she could have lifted the kind of hammer she'd have needed to do the job. And don't get ideas about hand jacks and all the rest of that. The Downtown Church is a very well-heeled little organization. They've got money and they've got connections. The police took that door apart, and about six independent laboratories did tests on it. Findings consistent with hand delivery. It's too bad her husband was in Tulsa at the time."

"Why?"

"Because he makes Marvelous Marvin Hagler look like a shrimp. Take your shower."

I grabbed my robe from the pile of clothes I'd unearthed from my suitcase the night before, and headed for the bathroom.

I have the kind of mind that can speculate about anything when it wants to, but almost never wants to when it should. In the bathroom, tucking my hair under a shower cap—I'd washed it the night before; I didn't want to wait two hours for it to dry—I speculated about Tempesta Stewart. From the skewed perspective of my very much not born-again life, it was hard to understand why she'd do what Nick said she'd done. I could accept the idea that her public persona could be just as calculated, and therefore just as manufactured, as Phoebe's, but the commonplace reason for doing something like that—to sell more books—didn't make sense in this case. I remembered the rise of Tempesta Stewart very well. Her books had started charting long before anybody ever heard anything about guerrilla tactics in defense of the Lord, and she'd been getting all the ink she needed when she'd been just the *only* romance writer whose novels would not be occasions of sin for the women of the Pentecostal and fundamentalist elite. In fact, the impression I had was that all this Christian-terrorism business was hurting her sales rather than helping them. It went over big with the readers of *Christian Soldiers Today,* but it made everybody else nervous. And for a while there, Tempesta had looked like the first self-styled Christian writer with a chance to break out into the general market.

My mind skittered through a whole list of increasingly unlikely explanations. Tempesta thought she'd heard from God Himself about the direction her life was supposed to take, and this was it. That was unlikely because, from what I understood, these people always told you when God had spoken to them, and Tempesta had never claimed any such thing. Everything I could think of was unlikely for just that reason, except the possibility that Tempesta was going off the deep end. She didn't seem to be. These people talked. They talked and talked and talked. They said anything that came into their heads, claimed the most amazing adventures, and then got offended if you refused to believe them. If Tempesta had stuck to seeing visions of Jesus in her bathroom mirror or hearing the Voice of God on her radio when the set was turned off, the whole thing would have made perfect sense. So would a Tempesta who actually was committing "revolutionary Christian acts," because there were people like that in the world and they did do things like that. "Militant Pro-Life Group Bombs Florida Clinic, Injures Six." What didn't make sense was a Tempesta Stewart who wasn't bombing abortion clinics but just cutting into her sales by saying she was.

Of course, the incident with the Downtown Church of Wicca might have been an anomaly, but I was willing to bet it wasn't. One of the things I'd found out in three years of being involved with crazy people was that anyone who had committed a really odd act once had probably either committed it before or was about to commit it again. The vandalism at the Downtown Church of Wicca might have been her first foray into terrorist fantasy, but it certainly wouldn't have been her last.

I dropped my robe, stared into the mirror—and came to a screeching halt. Instant replay: the mirror, the nattering worry about wrinkles, my hands. I put my hands up to the light and looked down at the creases between the fingers and the palms. I didn't expect to see anything. When I'd found those blue lines the night before, I'd gone back out into the room to talk to Nick about them. I'd found him snoring. I'd thought about waking him up and decided not to. He'd had as long a day as I had. I couldn't think of a thing he could do. It had seemed silly to disturb him for an exercise in futility. I'd gone back into the bathroom, climbed into the shower and taken special care washing off my hands.

Now the blue lines were still there—fainter, like washed blue ink, but there. I got back into my robe and went out to the main part of the room.

"Nick," I said. "Look at this."

He had stacked his papers away and was combing his hair, bending over nearly double to get a look at his face in the vanity mirror. He turned when I came in and stared at my outstretched hands.

"You look like Lady Macbeth walking," he said. "Look at what?"

"This." I shoved a hand at him and pointed to the lines in the creases with the index finger of the other one. The light in the bedroom was weaker than the light in the bathroom. I moved closer to the lamp so he could get a better look.

"Ink," he said positively. "You're letting pens explode in your bag again."

"I don't think so. It was there last night. I've got it on both hands. And when I found it last night, it was—I don't know. Powdery. Gritty. Like eye shadow that had been sweated into and gone all gunky."

"Eye shadow?"

"What really worries me about this," I said, "is that Mrs. Keeley had the same sort of thing on her last night. I mean she may have, of course, because I only saw it from a distance. But just under her ear on one side she had a streak of something I thought was blue eye shadow, and I remember thinking it didn't make any sense, because Mrs. Keeley would never use eye shadow."

"Maybe it was somebody else's eye shadow. Maybe that's your eye shadow."

"I don't wear eye shadow either. And eye shadow would have come right off. I can't seem to get this stuff washed out."

Nick sat back and rubbed his face. Then he laughed a little. "You know," he said, "if this was 1933, I might actually have an explanation for you. Although how the hell you'd have gotten hold of it—"

"Gotten hold of what?"

"This kind of chalk." He stood up and stretched, habitual restlessness. "In the thirties they used to dust the things they gave to kidnappers, like leather bags or newspapers they wrapped money in, with this kind of chalk. It was colorless when it was dry, but when you sweated into it it turned colors. Blue sometimes. Green. Anyway, the idea was, the kidnappers would pick up their loot and get this stuff all over their hands, and it would be the devil's own business to get the color off. Then the police would pick up the suspects and look at their hands, and they'd know."

"They stopped doing that? It sounds like a great idea."

"It wasn't. In the first place, it didn't work all that well with hands. It turned out you had to sweat a lot before the stuff actually started to work, and there had to be a lot of the chalk, too. And the chalk would just flake off whatever you put it on, so by the time the kidnappers got to the money there might not be enough of the stuff left to do any good. And if there was enough, it was even worse. Kidnappers are not nice people, McKenna. They'd find their hands turning blue or green or whatever, and they'd kill their victim and just hide out until the color wore off."

"Oh," I said.

"I think they still make the stuff, but they use it for structural engineering problems. You know, you're building a skyscraper and you've got floor after floor but no walls, and you have to put some of the partitions in before you close off. You need something you can mark the lines with that won't wash away in a rainstorm and won't blur too much. This stuff turns out to be really good if you mix it with water first. DuraBond, I think it's called. Anyway, it's dirt cheap and easy to use. But I can't see when you'd have been in a building under construction. Or Mrs. Keeley either."

"I haven't been in a building under construction. Are you sure it isn't used for anything else?"

"It's hardly used for construction anymore. You can buy it in most hardware stores, if that's any help. I think do-it-yourself nuts like it. It's like I said, though. It's really old technology. There are new felt-tips on the market that—"

"Nick."

"Only trying to help."

"Maybe I'd better go take that shower."

I started for the bathroom, but I never got there. When Tempesta Stewart knocks on a door, she makes sure she's going to be heard.

# TWELVE

She came through the door jangling like an old-fashioned sleigh, the charms on her sterling-silver link bracelets clacking together every time she took a step. When I first met her, she'd gone in for a lot of gold. In the days before the public holiness of Jim and Tammy Bakker bit the dust, almost everybody I'd ever heard describe himself as "born again" went in for a lot of gold. In the wake of IRS audits, church secretaries with *Playboy* contracts and public confessions of the pursuit of lust, all that had gone out of style. Tempesta was loaded down, but not with anything I couldn't have afforded myself even in my leaner years. What she looked like was an upscale version of the Perfect American Housewife as she appears in ads in *Metropolitan Life* and *Architectural Digest*. It was a very different housewife look from the one cultivated by Hazel Ganz. It let you know Tempesta had money, or that her husband did. It could never in a million years have been described as either "homey" or "maternal." Her print skirt had come straight from Laura Ashley—a hundred fifteen dollars. Her blue blazer was cashmere. Even her high-heeled boots were designer items, although not the slap-in-the-face kind put out by Gucci. I looked them over and decided Susan Bennis Warren Edwards, Park Avenue. That was another thing about Tempesta. She could talk Southern all she wanted, she could prattle on forever about tending her garden and life back home on the farm, but she was essentially an urban woman. She would have looked right at home at the reception desk in any law firm on Wall Street.

She came into the foyer, looked me up and down with undisguised contempt, looked Nick up and down with resignation and planted herself in the chair Nick had been sitting in when she knocked. Then she rooted through her bag until she found a pack of cigarettes and a silver lighter and lit up.

"I keep trying to quit these things, but it never works," she said.

"My husband says they're the work of the devil, and for once I believe him."

"For once?" I said.

"I told you," she said, "don't start. I've had enough today." She looked at Nick. "I suppose you told her *all about* the witch's door?"

"It depends what you mean by 'all about,'" Nick said.

"I'd tell you the truth again, which is that God gave me the strength to do it, but you wouldn't believe it anyway. And that's not what this is about. Are you two living in sin?"

I had just got a cigarette of my own going. I choked on the smoke. "Tempesta," I said.

But Tempesta wasn't looking at me. She was looking at Nick, and the way she was looking at him was oddly refreshing. I had never met a woman, even a woman who calls herself a lesbian, who does not look at Nick with a certain amount of sexual speculation. Nick is that kind of man. Like Christopher Sarandon or the young Peter Fonda, he would make the perfect romance-novel hero. As far as Tempesta was concerned, he might as well have been Moe, Larry or Curly. She looked right through him.

"What I've heard," she said, "is that *she* is good at investigating things." She tossed her head in my direction. "In my opinion, the only things women are good at investigating are their credit-card limits, but I could always be wrong. With God, all things are possible. Not that I think *she's* found God."

"What was it you wanted Miss McKenna to investigate?"

"Oh, don't 'Miss McKenna' me. She wrote 'Ms.' on her bio anyway. What I want her to investigate is this." She stuck her hands back into her purse and came up with a plain white business envelope, her name scrawled across the front in blue ink. She tossed it on the vanity table. She blew smoke at it. "Take a look at that," she said. "The writing on the front is the desk clerk's. I asked. What's inside—well, take a look."

I picked the envelope up off the vanity table. It reminded me of something, but I couldn't remember what. I turned it over and saw that the flap had been tucked in, but not moistened and glued down. I pulled the flap out and found a folded piece of typing paper.

"Read it," Tempesta said.

I read it. It had been spelled out in thick red crayon, and what it

said was: YER AN ENEMY OF WOMIN EVERYWHERE. YER OUGHT TO BE
DEAD. I put it down.

It's one of the sad truths about being a writer, any kind of writer,
that books bring out the worst in nuts. A writer whose work deals with
violence, as mine does, has the hardest time, but no writer is completely immune. Phoebe had had a nut letter or two in her time.
Amelia had had dozens. This was awful, but I couldn't see that it had
anything to do with me.

"For God's sake," I said. "What were you talking about on the
phone? How could you think this had anything to do with me?"

"Why not?"

"Tempesta, this is hate mail. We all get hate mail from time to time.
If this is the first—"

"*She's* supposed to be good at investigating things," Tempesta inter-
rupted, turning to Nick. She turned back to me. "I've had my share of
hate mail," she said. "More than my share. Any human being who
does the Lord's work in this secular society gets hate mail. And on
some level that may be legitimate hate mail, but I will tell you what it
is *not*. It is *not* the work of some illiterate crazy."

"She's right," Nick said.

"She's right?" I said.

Tempesta snatched the letter back. "In the first place," she said,
"crayon it may be written in, but heavyweight bond is what it's written
*on*. Maybe you work on a computer, but I still use a typewriter, and I
use heavyweight bond for final drafts. The stuff costs an arm and a
leg. And feel this. It's excellent quality."

I took the letter back. Tempesta was right. It was excellent quality
—in fact, it was Southworth cockle finish, some of the best paper
made, and it did cost an arm and a leg. It also had a very distinctive
watermark.

Tempesta waited to make sure she'd made her point, then went on.
"In the second place," she said, "my husband gets letters from illiterate people every day of his life. He even gets them hand-delivered on
Sundays, after the service. He's a preacher, in case nobody's bothered
to tell you that. And contrary to what the Godless media is trying to
make the people of this country believe, not every Christian charis-
matic preacher is Jim Bakker. My husband reads his mail. I read his
mail. I answer a lot of it, too. I've never seen a letter where somebody

couldn't spell 'your' but got all the letters in 'ought' right. You know how ignorant people spell 'ought'? A-w-t. That's how. A-w-t."

"Jesus Christ," I said.

"Never mind the fact that whoever it is knows it should be 'an' and not just 'a' in front of 'enemy.'"

She caught the look I sent her and shrugged. "Among the other things I've done in my life, before I married the man God made for me and set down to write good books good Christian women could read, was teach. At Fayesboro Christian School. You wouldn't believe the things I saw at Fayesboro Christian School. These people would come barefoot out of the hills, they'd work themselves sick, they'd get a Ford dealership or a Kentucky Fried Chicken franchise and they'd think they were rich. And they still talked like they were calling hogs back in West Virginia. And their kids—"

"Shh," I said.

"Don't shush me," Tempesta said. "Nobody shushes me. Not even my husband."

"Wait a minute," I insisted.

I thought, hard. Ever since I'd arrived in Baltimore, I'd been so tired, I hadn't been able to concentrate. Even with all the sleep I'd had last night, I still felt fuzzy. Things happened, and seemed important, and then disappeared from my consciousness. Blue lines on my hands. Something Nick had said about a letter from the IRS. The desk clerk calling out to me as I walked Phoebe toward the elevators after checking in—

I looked around the room, still piled with steamer trunks and miscellaneous luggage. Nick had meant to move them that morning. He'd probably decided it would wake me up.

"Do you know where my tote bag is?" I asked him.

"This thing?" He held it up.

"Give it to me."

He tossed it over, and I rooted through the piles of ancient American Express bills and cat-clawed Lord and Taylor catalogues for the envelope I now remembered sticking away in there, more than twenty-four hours ago.

"When Phoebe and I checked in yesterday," I said, "the desk clerk handed me this—wait, here it is." I drew out the envelope. The similarities were unmistakable. Plain white. "Patience Campbell Mc-

Kenna" scrawled across the front in ink. I turned it over. The flap had been tucked in, but not glued. "How much you want to bet?" I said.

"I can't believe this," Tempesta said. "She actually looks happy about it."

"Open it," Nick said.

I opened it. Inside, there was a single sheet of heavyweight bond. I checked the watermark and found the Southworth symbol. The message was in black crayon this time. It said: YER RUIN IT FOR EVERBODY. YER OUGHT TO BE DEAD.

"Score," I said.

"Is she always like this?" Tempesta said. "Doesn't she realize what this means? That stupid woman got herself murdered, and as far as anybody knew, it was just some neighbor of hers. With this going on— you know this has got to be connected with that. You know it does. I mean, just one of us wouldn't have been, but two of us—"

"I don't see how the two things necessarily have to be connected," Nick said. "After all, you could be right. Mrs. Keeley could have been killed by practically anybody. I think it's highly unlikely the murderer would have been someone on the tour. Juxtaposition does not necessitate—"

I held up a hand. "Stop, both of you. You're both wrong. The murderer does have to be somebody on the tour, or somebody connected to it. I suppose it could be Gail Larson. But that was clear before we ever saw these letters. The letters don't exactly change anything. They just make it easier."

"Easier," Tempesta said. "She's gone off her head."

"Look," I said. "Mrs. Keeley's body was found in Gail Larson's bookstore. Right? The bookstore was locked between two and about quarter to four. Gail had a key. Evelyn had a key. Mrs. — you know, I don't know that."

"Don't know what?" Nick said.

"That Mrs. Keeley didn't have a key. I just assumed she didn't. She and Evelyn were supposed to meet at the store. Gail didn't like the woman—Mrs. Keeley, I mean. You know what she was like. If I had been Gail, I wouldn't have put it past her to get a duplicate made if she had the chance. That's just about all Gail would have needed. That woman drove her nuts. And Phoebe said something yesterday about seeing Mrs. Keeley on the street somewhere, checking her watch and looking like she was waiting for somebody who was late."

"And you think it was Evelyn," Nick said.

"There's a way to find out." I got up and went back to the bed, to the night table and the phone. I picked up and put in a call to The Butler Did It. "It's after eleven o'clock," I said. "If Gail isn't actually open, she'll probably be there cleaning up the mess. Unless the police are still— Hello?"

"I'm not open," Gail Larson said. "I may never be open. If you'll please—"

"Calm down," I said.

"Pay?"

"Hi," I said. "I thought I'd call on the off chance the police were finished with the place."

There was a sound in the background like the rustling of a thousand doves. It was probably paper. One of the things I'd noticed, around the time Barbara Defborn and I went out for a drink, was that hundreds of paperback books seemed to have been accidentally trashed in the crisis.

The rustling stopped and was replaced by a clanking. I hadn't the faintest idea what that was. Then the clanking stopped and Gail said, "Okay. I can talk. I had to do something with this chair. It keeps collapsing. You have no idea what kind of mess this place is in. And your Christopher Brand was right. Everybody from Alexandria to Wilmington wants to drop in at the store."

"Don't you have any help?"

"Not today. Oh God, Pay. I thought it would be slow. I gave everybody the afternoon off and now they've completely disappeared. Don't they read the papers?"

"I don't read the papers."

"Never mind. Is this about something in particular?"

I ignored the impatience in her voice. She was right to feel it, but I figured I was just as right not to feel guilty about it. After all, this *was* about something in particular.

"What I wanted to know was, did you give a key to the store to Mrs. Harold?"

The quality of the silence changed almost instantaneously. I could practically feel the freeze.

"Dear *God,*" Gail exploded. "You and that Defborn woman. I must be getting a reputation as some kind of lunatic. What do you people take me for? I didn't even want Margaret Keeley in this place without a chaperon. She'd have gone through my drawers. Hell, she got herself into the back room and tried to do that a couple of times while I was actually here. She read people's credit-card receipts, I'm not kidding—"

"So Evelyn was supposed to let her in," I said.

"Of course Evelyn was supposed to let her in. That was part of the deal. I think I dreamed up some nonsense about how it was Evelyn's show and she'd feel all huffy if anybody else had a key. *I* don't know. I was just talking. And—"

She was going on, but I wasn't listening. I have my flashes of insight, but I'm not really that quick a study, most of the time. A lifetime of reading and writing fiction has made me capable of periodic mental leaps, but it's an acquired skill. Whatever talent for deduction I've earned a reputation for is the result of sheer, plodding, elementary logic. Logic was kicking in now. I could picture Gail standing next to me while I sat on a mantel in the store, with one corner of the room occupied by cops and "support personnel," telling me that when she'd come in that afternoon, *all* of Mrs. Keeley's work was done, but *none* of Evelyn's was.

"Gail?" I said.

"Sorry," Gail said.

"No need to apologize," I said. "Just one more thing. This party, did you get to plan the details yourself, or did Evelyn draw up a blueprint?"

"Well, I wouldn't exactly call it a blueprint," Gail said. "Evelyn sent me all this stuff about two months ago, the most detailed plans I've ever seen for a signing in my life. It would've sent me right up the wall, but there was a note attached to it, and the note said not to worry. It was all going to fall apart when we actually got into it and she wouldn't care. She'd just feel better if there was a master plan somewhere. Even if she knew we wouldn't follow it."

"That sounds like Evelyn."

"Yeah, well. It was a big project. When I'm being sane, I don't blame her. I'd probably be a lot better off if I got a little more organized myself."

"How master was this master plan?" I said. "Did it have a signing schedule?"

"Oh, yeah. But that was the least part of it. Evelyn said she'd set up schedules for every part of the tour, trying to give each of you a shot at the best spots, but the way you guys were, it almost never worked out. She said you people were always bumping each other around, and *nobody* could talk manners into Amelia Samson. She was right, too."

"I know she was. Who was supposed to be up first last night?"

There was a pause. "You know," Gail said slowly, "that's a funny thing. It never struck me before. Everything was such a mess and I couldn't find any books and nobody knew where Evelyn was, but it almost worked out the way it was supposed to."

"I was supposed to sign first," I said.

"Exactly," Gail said. "Isn't that a coincidence?"

"I don't know. Did you ever find the rest of the books?"

"About half an hour ago. They were way in the back. Under about a jillion other boxes. I don't even know how they got there. They were *under* boxes that came in weeks ago."

"Right," I said.

"Are you okay?" Gail said. "You sound funny."

"I'm fine. Maybe I'll stop over later this evening."

I hung up and looked back across the room. Tempesta and Nick were standing side by side in front of the vanity table, staring at me as if I'd lost my mind—or maybe as if they expected me to pull a rabbit out of a hat. I had a terrible feeling I might be able to manage the latter.

"I have just," I told them, "had the scariest hunch I've ever had in my life."

# THIRTEEN

By the time we were all in the hall on our way to Tempesta's room, I had begun to sympathize with her feeling that I must be crazy. I have always loved puzzles. Both my bedroom and my office, back in New York, were littered with collections of crosswords and Double-Crostics. I've had a subscription to *Games* magazine since the day it first appeared. I get a little package from Will Weng's Crossword Club in the mail every month. In recent years, I've even begun to develop a passion for murder mysteries of the classic 1930s type: Agatha Christie, Dorothy L. Sayers, Ellery Queen. Sometimes my life and the situation I'm in begin to seem like scenes from those. Whenever that happens, I *am* good at figuring things out, just the way I'm good at doing logic puzzles. (I haven't won the *Games* national crossword competition yet, but I'm working on it.) It's a matter of believing that there are no consequences. Sitting in my room with Tempesta and Nick, going through the elements that had been perking through my brain as I slept, putting it all together, I had felt less anxiety—less *pressure*—than I did when I had just delivered a manuscript.

Going down that hall was something else again. I kept thinking I must have slept very well, because the particulars had arranged themselves very neatly in my brain. I'd only needed an organizing principle. Her note, and my own, gave me that. I couldn't have explained it the night before, but I'd known from the beginning that Margaret Keeley's murderer had to be one of us—a member of the tour, or someone (like Gail Larson) connected to it. Part of that was an assumption I'd only recently had verified—that Gail had *not* given Mrs. Keeley a key to the store—but it had been an assumption based on sound knowledge. Without a key, Mrs. Keeley would have had to be let into the store. Gail could have done it if she were there. Evelyn could have done it if she and Margaret met somewhere, even just on the street in front of the store. At that point, anyone who wanted to murder Margaret

Keeley and leave her body in The Butler Did It had a problem. Someone who had *nothing* to do with the signing party would have looked
conspicuous hanging around North Charles Street. The store was
closed. There was also the body itself. At least *part* of the reason for
sticking it under that table and covering it with the cloth had to be to
delay discovery. Anyone but Evelyn would have had to worry about
both Evelyn and Gail messing around that table, setting up. The only
way to avoid that was to set it up the way it was supposed to be. I
thought whoever had killed Margaret Keeley had probably been a little
nervous about time. Or else . . .

I stopped at Tempesta's door and stared at the knob as if it were a
piece of nonrepresentational art. Behind me, Tempesta and Nick
came to a halt. Tempesta let out a noise that sounded remarkably like
"shit," surprising both because it was a word I'd never heard her use
(she said "doo-doo" on cable television) and because up until then she
had made no sound at all. No one had. For the entire length of our
trip, the only audible evidence of our existence had been the soft
*shoosh* of leather on carpet.

I turned around, aware that I was stalling and not caring very much.
It really is different when the consequences begin to appear plain. I no
more wanted to walk into Tempesta's room at that moment than I
wanted to take a high dive off the World Trade Center.

"You know," I said, "all this time, I've been assuming the business
with the books was a stopgap thing. Sort of second best. I thought
whoever it was had killed Mrs. Keeley and then tried to rig things so
she wouldn't be found, but there was a time problem and it couldn't
be done the way it should have been. I thought the books should have
been out of their cartons and all set up. That way, there'd be *absolutely
no chance* that someone would extract them and go over to that table
to make a display of them and accidentally stumble on the body. Then
I thought there probably hadn't been time for that—or the killer
thought there hadn't been time—and so he or she just moved things
around in the back. Now I wonder—"

"McKenna," Nick said patiently. "If we're going to go in there—"

"In a minute," I said. I had my hand on the knob. It felt slick. "The
thing is, once you start working it out, what actually did happen makes
more sense. Gail was able to find my books last night, and only my
books. She said on the phone that when she found the other boxes

they were buried under returns and shipments and God knows what else. With all the confusion last night, they were effectively out of the picture. And I can't honestly say the time element works either. Those book boxes are heavy, especially when they're full of hardcovers, and most of the ones for the charity sale were. Hazel Ganz and Ivy Samuels Tree and Lydia only come out in paperback, but everybody else— Christopher Brand, Amelia, Phoebe, Tempesta here—had at least one box of the heavy stuff. Amelia could have moved those boxes in a hurry. Christopher Brand might have been able to. The rest of us—"

"Christopher Brand," Tempesta said, almost spitting. "Gail Larson *asked* him to help with those boxes last night, but he wouldn't do it. Oh, he told her he'd do it. He isn't a complete turd. He just disappeared as soon as he'd said yes."

"I wish I could be sure that was significant," I said. "Unfortunately, it sounds just like Christopher Brand."

"Turd," Tempesta repeated helpfully.

"Don't you think we ought to go in if we're going?" Nick said.

Tempesta brushed past him, pushed me aside and went to the door. It unlocked with a computer card instead of an ordinary key, for which I'd been grateful for all of my stay. The hotel in New Orleans had had ordinary keys. I'd never actually managed to get through my door by myself. If Phoebe and I were together, she got us in. If I was alone, and Phoebe out, I had to call the desk to get someone to work the thing for me.

Tempesta pushed the door open, hesitated and then walked in ahead of us. I wondered what her hesitation was about. I didn't wonder about my own.

I came in last, after Nick, and looked around. Tempesta's room was a clone of my own, except that her wall of windows looked out on what appeared to be a cluster of other buildings, instead of the harbor. That didn't matter particularly. The weather was so bad, it was the only view in town.

Tempesta got out her cigarettes again. "Here it is," she said. "What you expect to find in it, I don't know."

I knew what I expected to find, but as I looked around I began to doubt I would. There was no mess of luggage here. Tempesta's single suitcase was lying on the far bed, open and empty. Through her open closet door, I could see a long hanger rod barely occupied by the perfect pack-light travel wardrobe. There was a multiple skirt hanger with five of Tempesta's favorite print dirndls on it. There were two other cashmere blazers, in navy blue and white. There were six white shirts with high collars still in their dry-cleaning plastic wrap. On the floor were four pairs of shoes, laid out with precision in a Prussian line.

I walked over to the closet and looked inside. Nothing.

"Did you go out this morning?" I asked Tempesta.

"Of course I went out," Tempesta said. "How do you think the bed got made? Maids hate to work with people in the rooms. How do you think I got that note? I picked it up in the lobby, of course."

"Did you get a call about it?"

"A call about it?"

"When hotel clerks have messages for guests, they usually set the message light blinking on the room phone. You call them up and they tell you to come down and get your envelope."

"I *know* that," Tempesta said. "I'm a Christian, not a hick. And no, there was no message light on on the phone. I checked last night and I didn't get a call this morning."

"How long were you gone?" I felt foolish, but I had to do it. I got down on my hands and knees and looked under the bed.

"I was gone about an hour," she said. I could just *feel* the odd look she was giving me. "I just went down to have breakfast. I brought my manuscript with me. It's due in a couple of weeks. I never got to work on it, though. I ran into Amelia Samson, and you know what Amelia is like. She spent the whole time babbling about the sorry state of romance fiction and then Hazel Ganz came along and started lecturing me about warranty clauses."

"Did you pick the note up before or after breakfast?"

"After." She bit her lip. "You know, I don't think it was there before breakfast. I spent all yesterday morning making conversation with that clerk they've got down there. She knows me. I passed her when I first came down and said good morning, and she never said a thing about a note."

"But she did when you were on your way back?"

"Yes. Of course, she might just have forgotten. And I must say, I thought this was a good hotel, but how they could let something like this go on—"

"Tempesta, no decent hotel reads its guests' private messages. Don't be absurd."

"But *this* kind of thing—"

"Death threats don't smell any differently than love letters," I said. "The clerks could probably get canned for invading the guests' privacy. If I knew one had invaded mine, I'd demand he get canned."

"Do you intend to lie on the floor forever?"

I got up, brushing off the part of my robe that had been in contact with the carpet, although it didn't need it. The vacuum cleaners that hotel used must have been the next-best thing to black holes.

"This doesn't make sense," I said.

"It surely doesn't," Tempesta said. "But *that's* all right. None of you people make sense. If I'd had any idea, when I was voted onto the board—"

"Tempesta, if you had any idea about anything, you'd have to join a convent. Have you been in your bathroom since you got upstairs?"

"I haven't even been in here," she said. "I got that note and read it in the lobby. I called you from there."

I went down her entrance foyer and into her bathroom, a clean white place that smelled pleasantly of sachet. The Inner Harbor was the only Sheraton I'd ever stayed at, but if they were all like this, I thought the chain must be doing pretty well. The smell of sachet. A shine on the floor that would have made my mother proud—and my mother is one of those women who insist on bathroom floors clean enough to do neurosurgery on. I walked over to the bathtub and pulled back the shower curtain. Nothing.

"McKenna?" Nick came up behind me.

"There isn't a single place to hide anything in in here," I said. "I can't believe it."

"There are a million places to hide something," Nick said. "Depending on what you want to hide. Look at all that closet space. Look at all those cabinets."

"Spaces aren't big enough." I sat down on the edge of the bathtub. Now that the danger of imminent revelation was past, both my anxiety and my panic were draining out of me. The whole thing felt like a logic puzzle again. I reached into the pocket of my robe for my cigarettes—Tempesta was smoking herself, after all—and got one out.

"It's got to be here somewhere," I said. "It doesn't make sense any other way."

"What doesn't make sense?" Nick said.

"She *never* makes sense," Tempesta said. "It's like I said before. None of them do."

I ignored her. "Assume that what did happen was supposed to happen," I said, pretending I was talking only to Nick. "What did happen was that a note was delivered to me yesterday morning just as I started to come up to the room. It could have been there all along, but I'll bet if we ask the desk clerk we'll find it was left on the counter *after* I came in—"

"How could it be left on the counter? Somebody must have spoken to the clerk. The clerk wrote your name on it," Nick said.

"Okay," I said. "Somebody may have spoken to the clerk, but I bet it didn't happen that way. Maybe someone handed it to a bellboy or just put it in my box—"

"There were clerks working back there," Nick objected. "There were people standing in line waiting to register."

"There weren't either by the time I got that note," I said. "That's a very efficient check-in operation they've got down there. We came in. Three people appeared out of nowhere to check us in. The line dispersed almost immediately. Phoebe was at the very end of it and she was done almost as soon as I was. We'll have to check it out, but I'm pretty sure that after everybody was taken care of, the clerks went to the back again. And stayed there until they were needed."

"Meaning someone could have gone around the counter and put something—where? I didn't see pigeonholes."

"There'll be something," I said. "Trust me. There has to be. Anyway, after that a clerk came through and found it and gave it to me, but it didn't really matter if it happened then. I could have got it anytime before the party." I poked my head past him to get a better look at Tempesta. "What do you usually do with hate mail?" I asked her.

"You mean genuine hate mail?" she said. "I do what you do with it. If there's an actual death threat, I call the cops."

"Exactly," I said. "And if I hadn't been so damn tired, I'd have called the cops, too. And then, later on, when I found the body, it would all look connected."

"Like somebody had it in for you and had gone really nuts," Nick said. He brightened. "Not bad. But how could he be sure you'd find the body?"

"I keep telling you," I said. "It was rigged that way. That's what I meant about the books. Gail said there was a schedule for the signings, but Evelyn didn't put much faith in it, because Christopher and Amelia and—other people—were always jockeying for position and messing the whole thing up. What the murderer did was make sure this couldn't be messed up. I was the best target. The Butler Did It is a mystery specialty bookstore. Gail carries my books on a regular basis. She *doesn't* normally carry anything by anyone else on the tour. Even if none of the books could be found right away, I'd be the likeliest one to sign first, because at least *some* of my stuff would be available. Then he moved things around in the back room so Gail really couldn't lay hands on anybody else's work. And there I was."

"And here *we* are," Tempesta said. "And as you can see, the room is empty. If you expected to find a body in it, you should have told me. *I* would have told *you* it wasn't possible."

"Even though you hadn't been back here since breakfast?"

"Patience, this is a *good hotel.* You said so yourself. The maid must have come in as soon as I left the room this morning. And the door was locked."

"There was yesterday," I said. "You were out yesterday. Phoebe was out, too. She saw you sitting in some storefront religious center."

"The American Army for Christ the King. Yes, I was out yesterday. I was out all afternoon. Do you really think I could have failed to find a body between then and now? In *here?*"

"No," I said. I wasn't happy about it.

Tempesta sighed. "I think your theory is just lovely, but I think it's all bunk. There's a flaw in your reasoning somewhere. Whoever killed Mrs. Keeley, it wasn't one of us. What reason would we have? And the letters—Christopher Brand, take my word for it."

"I never said the letters hadn't come from Christopher Brand."

"That man hates every woman who won't commit an indecent act with him. Now, if you *don't* mind, I have things to do today. I have a car running up a parking bill—"

"Car?" I said. A light went on in my head. Tempesta had a note. A body had to be hidden *somewhere.*

"Oh boy," Nick said.

"You may want to spend your time in this city chasing after buses and hailing cabs, but I have work to do. I rented a very nice little Mazda." Tempesta smirked. "I know a very good rental agency in this city. A *Christian* one. You'd be amazed how much easier your life gets once you accept Jesus Christ as your personal savior."

I must have spaced out for a minute there. The next thing I remember is Nick grabbing my arm and shaking it, pumping away just above my elbow as if he wanted to break it off. The same light that had gone off in my head had gone off in his.

"McKenna," he kept saying. "McKenna, go get dressed. We'll meet you downstairs."

I went back to my room. I pulled on an old pair of jeans and a turtleneck and one of Nick's best sweaters. I went downstairs. I even almost got lost. For some reason, I couldn't talk myself out of the idea that Tempesta had parked her Christian car in the Sheraton's garage. She'd told me otherwise. I should have known better.

By the time I got there, the trunk was standing open and Nick was beside it, looking angry. There was no sign of Tempesta, but I knew she had to be somewhere on the phone, calling Barbara Defborn back to us.

I walked up and peered into the thing. The light was dim. The bulbs and fixtures overhead were filmed with grease. There were no windows. I sent up a heartfelt thanksgiving that it was so difficult to see. The lighting at The Butler Did It the night before had been strong enough to shoot a movie in. I can do without that kind of clarity when I'm looking at a corpse.

Stuffed into the trunk, folded and twisted and packed down so it would fit, was the body of Evelyn Nesbitt Kleig.

On the small patch of skin under her earlobe and above her jaw was a thick slash of blue.

# FOURTEEN

All crime scenes, like all murders, are alike. That may seem like a ridiculous statement—what in the name of God does a Mafia execution have in common with a domestic homicide?—but there's more truth to it than anyone but a cop realizes. Barring the essentially accidental, like a deer rifle that goes off in the middle of a family argument, murderers all think the same. The only difference between the mental machinations of a Mafia hit man and a wife who kills her husband for his insurance is in their assumptions about the inevitability of habit. The Mafia hit man accepts that killing is something that has to be done again and again. The wife convinces herself she will need to do it only once. Both of them believe in the justice of what they're doing. Both of them are convinced the cops are stupid. Neither of them realizes that self-defense is not an infinitely elastic concept.

For a while after the forensic team arrived, I sat on a concrete abutment in a corner, feeling as if I'd wandered into some cosmic version of an infinite loop. The garage had been empty when I first arrived, but it had filled up quickly. Tempesta's car had been parked at ground level and people had wandered in off the street in droves. The sight of them blocking the entrance and exit ramps made the place feel claustrophobic, as small and overstuffed as The Butler Did It had been during the investigation. The arc lamps made me think of Margaret Keeley. The arc lamps are portable. They are the property of the police department. It makes sense that they get packed up and carted around to wherever they are needed. For some reason, when I see them standing and lit, I can't help thinking of them as permanent additions to whatever territory they've invaded.

I reached into my pocket for cigarettes, realized I had a young patrolman staring at my hand, and left the pack abandoned in my jeans. Cops hate smoking at crime scenes. The only reason I'd been allowed to get away with it the night before was that, in the confusion, no one had noticed me. Stray cigarette butts are evidence. If an investigator or an innocent spectator leaves one near a dead body, it has to be followed up just as carefully as any real clue. It wastes everybody's time and everybody's money, and it's the easiest thing in the world to guard against. Long before the Surgeon General found cause to label packs of Marlboro menthols dangerous, police departments all across America were establishing no-smoking sections of their own.

I went to sit on the abutment after I'd talked to Barbara Defborn, meaning after I was free to leave. I knew she assumed I *wouldn't* leave. God only knew, I'd hung around until the bitter end the night before. Barbara Defborn's mind worked the way it had to—like a good policewoman's, which was what she was. To her, a crime scene was like a back garden plot planted for a treasure hunt. It was full of little chips of silver and gold, waiting to be found, and pored over, and stored for future use. She liked fabric threads and stray hairs and finger-oil smudges on the waxed surfaces of painted metal. All those things meant something to her. They did not, however, mean anything to me.

"It's going to be too close to tell," she'd said when she was ushering me out of the garage owner's cramped little office and giving me permission to go, "but I'll bet this one was killed first. I'll just bet."

"I will, too," I said. "The times add up that way, when people saw her, when they didn't. And I don't think she ever got to the store. None of her work was done."

"At least this time we've got a car," she said. "Cars are a lot better to work with. Especially rental cars. They get vacuumed out regularly. Whatever we find in that trunk is likely to be pertinent, and we're going to *find*."

I murmured something that amounted to an expression of polite interest and moved away. I was cold and sweaty at the same time. Like most tiered garages, this one guarded against employee suffocation by having concrete walls that went only halfway up each story. Wind and rain and cold came pouring through the oversized cracks, drenching the hoods of the cars that were parked along the perimeters and making the oil-slick asphalt underfoot look clean. The place smelled anyway—of carbon monoxide and raw gasoline, of human sweat and the acrid dryness that warns of space heaters left on too long. It was a thoroughly uncomfortable place, and I wanted more than anything to be out of it.

After a while, I stood up, went to the wall and looked out to the street. I was at the bottom of a gently sloping ramp, not quite level with the pavement. I tried to see through the moving masses of umbrellas and raincoats to something that might be Nick. Nick had been the person Barbara talked to first, maybe because she hadn't had a chance to talk to him before. When he was finished and I was on my way to getting started, I asked him to go back to the hotel and find Phoebe and Adrienne. All I needed was to have Adrienne hear about this on the radio, or from some stranger in the hotel's lobby. I still wasn't sure how I was going to get her through the trouble she already knew we were in.

I stood on tiptoe, grabbed the top of the half-wall and leaned out as far as I could go. Nick was nowhere in sight, but even with rain drenching my hair I felt I'd manufactured myself an advantage. For one thing, I could breathe. It might be cold on the streets of Baltimore, and wet, but it wasn't suffocating. They seemed to be doing a better than fair job of keeping the pollution problem under control. For another thing, as long as I was leaning out, I couldn't see back in. Every time I looked back in, I got a clear view of the bulletproof plastic front wall of the manager's office, and through it of the wall at the back. That one was plastered floor to ceiling and side to side with bumper stickers that said HONK IF YOU LOVE JESUS.

The weight of the rain and the strength of the wind dragged a large part of my hair across my eyes. I winced against the sting and clawed at it, pulling it back. I tucked it under the collar of Nick's sweater, soaking my shirt. Then I started rubbing my eyes to get the water out.

When I was finally able to see again, the street looked different. I went through all the usual explanations—thinner traffic, people getting in out of the weather, a change in the luminosity of streetlamps—and came up dissatisfied. Even if all those things had happened, I probably wouldn't have noticed a difference. I am a noticing person, but not in quite that way. I turned my head from side to side, checking out different colors and styles in rain boots. I looked down at the police car blocking the garage's entrance and cutting off my view to the north. I started to look away again and stopped.

The police car was still where it had been when I'd first started

looking over the halfway, but the two policemen weren't. They had
been inside their vehicle, safely out of the wet. Now they were standing on the pavement at the very far edge of what I was able to see, and
it was obvious they'd got out there in a hurry. Baltimore police are
provided with those same space-agey rain suits police in New York
have. I'd seen half a dozen officers wearing them at Gail's. These two
hadn't waited to put theirs on. One of them—the short blond one—
hadn't even taken the time to grab his hat.

I hoisted myself up as far as I could go and leaned over until I was
about to pitch onto the heads of passing pedestrians. Nothing. I lowered myself back into the garage and looked at the ramp I was standing on. Height or distance, that was the decision. I was never the
world's best physics student. I couldn't remember which would give
me the better view of what I wanted to see.

I tried height first, proving one of the great principles of my life: I
always start out doing the wrong thing. All getting closer got me was
cut off completely. By the time I was halfway to the payout booth, I
couldn't see the police car or the entrance booth at all. I backed up
and went toward the opposite end of the room. The ramp's incline
started out gentle, but it got steeper almost immediately. I climbed all
the way to the turn and leaned over the wall again. I'd gone just far
enough.

Standing about five feet away from the two uniformed patrolmen
was a man in a heavy, oversized winter coat, his hair sticking up from
his head as if it had been greased and wired, his hands moving up and
down and up and down as if he were having a psychotic break. Every
stranger on the street probably thought he was a wino with the DTs
and maybe better than average luck at the Salvation Army store. He
looked like one. He behaved like one. His coat was so blatantly expensive, the cops were undoubtedly wondering where he'd stolen it.

I, of course, knew he was Jonathon Lowry.

I stuck my hands in my pockets, said a very rude word and headed
for the street.

If the cops had been where they belonged—meaning in their car,
guarding the entrance to the garage—I would never have gotten out
without being questioned. That's another prime rule of scene-of-the-
crime investigation. You never let anyone you don't know get away

from you. When I came down the entrance ramp, the cops were still busy with Jon. I could have moved Patton's Third Army into that place without anybody official noticing.

A crowd of spectators had begun to form, stopping pedestrian traffic in both directions. I weasled through the sparse line at the back—it was, after all, raining hard enough to cause flash floods—and came to a stop behind the short blond policeman. The taller one had moved forward a little, as if he'd had enough of this. He probably thought Jon was getting violent.

Jon was as violent as I'd ever seen him, or ever expected to—which meant not very. He was hopping from foot to foot, the hops getting shorter and less frequent as the water soaked into his coat and made it heavier. Every once in a while he shouted something, mostly made incoherent by the wind. I heard "You'd let me in if she were my wife" and "All I want is to know what's going on," but nothing else.

I tapped the short blond policeman on the shoulder and said, "Excuse me."

"Police business," the officer said, not bothering to turn around. "We have this situation under control."

"I'm sure you do," I said, "but I'm Patience Campbell McKenna. I was just in there talking to Barbara Defborn."

That got his attention. He swung his head around and gave me that look new men give me so often, and that I try to ignore. He seemed to be trying to decide if I was a figment of his imagination. Six feet tall. A hundred twenty-five pounds. Big blue eyes. Honey blond. I had to be kidding.

Five feet away, Jon Lowry stopped hopping, stuck his neck out as far as it would go and blinked. "Patience!" he said. "Patience! You tell them! You tell them they have to let me in there!"

The taller of the two turned toward me then. "You know this guy?"

"Slightly," I said.

Jon Lowry ran straight toward us, blasting through the arm the taller policeman put out to stop him without even noticing it was there.

"God, I hate this," he said. "It's just like my bankers. Just like them. Everybody knows what's good for me. Everybody knows what I ought to be doing. Christopher Brand said she was dead. Is she dead? She can't be dead. She was *immortal.*"

"Jon," I said.

"And *them,*" Jon said. He whirled around, flapped his arms at the cops and whirled back to me. "They're all the same, you know. People who've got official positions. They're all alike. God, you wouldn't believe what some of these assholes have done to me. Had me spied on. Had my apartment bugged. Did I tell you one of my lawyers had my apartment bugged? He did. I found the damn thing by accident. Think I'm crazy. *These* two idiots think I'm drunk."

"Are you?"

"Of course not. I just want—I just want—" He deflated so fast, he might never have been there at all. One minute he was all fire and energy and righteous indignation. The next he was staring at his shoes. "Is she dead?" he said. "Christopher said—but you know Christopher. Christopher will say anything."

"I'd like to know how Christopher knew," I said.

"It's true?"

"Jon—"

"Oh, never mind. Don't treat me like a two-year-old. I'm not a two-year-old. And I knew it was true. Christopher's a bastard, but he wouldn't make *up* something like that."

"I don't suppose he would," I said.

Jon pointed toward the garage. "I want to go in there," he said. "They can't keep me out, can they? I want to go in there and see her one more time."

I felt a tap on my shoulder and turned around to see the tall cop waiting to speak to me, looking polite and expectant and just as if I didn't have anything to do with this lunatic he'd run into. I told Jon to wait a minute and edged off. I know a signal for a private conversation when I see one.

The tall one had about an inch on me. He glanced over my shoulder to make sure Jon was staying put and said, "He says he's Jonathon Hancock Lowry, that billionaire guy. Is he?"

"He certainly is."

"Shit," the officer said. "Excuse my language. But—shit."

"I don't think you have to worry about the usual sort of trouble," I said. "He doesn't know how to cause it. And God only knows he looks just like what you thought he was."

"A nut," the officer said.

"At least a bum," I said.

The tall officer shook his head. "I've been looking at bums all my life. I used to have vagrancy detail when there still was such a thing. I can smell cheap booze a hundred miles away. I thought he was a schizo."

This time, I was the one who looked back to be sure Jon was staying put. If there was one thing I'd learned about Jon Lowry on this tour, it was that you didn't throw the word "schizo" around in his presence unless you really wanted to cause trouble. His crazy Aunt Gertrude had been "schizo."

"Look," the tall officer said. "I'm not going to do anything here. I'm not going to haul him in. I'm not even going to go on telling him he can't go in there. Hell, if he was as close to that woman as he's been trying to make us believe, Defborn would probably love to talk to him. Woman yaps her life away anyway. *But,* and this is my big *but,* in general, what we've found is, it's not so good to let relatives and close friends get a look at a corpse unless they've already seen it. If you know what I mean."

"You mean unless they're the ones who made it," I said.

"Yeah," the officer said.

"Well, I don't think he made this one. He was—never mind. That's not proof anyway. I'll talk to him."

"Talk him out of going up there. At least until the body's out."

"I'll try."

"Shit," the officer said, "any other time, I'd be trying to get him in there. Just to make sure she could question him before he got away. But she says—"

"We're all safely ensconced in the hotel," I said. "He isn't going anywhere at the moment. I'll get him out of here."

"Good. And in the meantime, try to explain to him that all acting like a crazy is going to get him is locked up. You hadn't come along, another five minutes we'd have taken him out for observation."

"He's just a little distraught," I said.

"Shit."

He stalked away from us, and climbed back into his cruiser. His partner followed.

"Patience?" Jon said.

I went up the street to him, wishing like hell that Jon had decided to stage this little drama somewhere sensibly protected from the rain. I was as thoroughly soaked as if I'd jumped fully clothed into a pool. I had been able to ignore the weather as long as the fireworks were going on, but now I was miserable. And wet. And achy. I was sure I felt a cold coming on.

I took Jon's arm and started to edge him, gently, toward the hotel. "Come on," I said. "Let's get in out of the cold. I need a drink."

Jon stood his ground. "Did that policeman tell you I was crazy?"

"No," I said. "He told me it wasn't a good idea for you to go in there, especially if you were who you said you were—"

"Jonathon Hancock Lowry, boy billionaire?"

"Jon Lowry, friend of the deceased. He was right, Jon. That's nothing for you to see. Believe me. Let's go back to the hotel, and have a drink, and calm down. All right?"

Jon Lowry folded his arms across his chest, stuck out his lip and said, "No."

# FIFTEEN

It would have been different if I'd won that argument. Winning always makes everything different. I've noticed that right along. In this case, I stood in the street with the rain pouring down on my head and rising in puddles at my feet, getting nowhere. I was also becoming more and more aware that the things I was seeing, when I took time away from Jon's ranting and his two-year-old insistence that everything had to go his way or not at all, lacked context—at least for me. I know New York well enough to pick the usual from the extraordinary, the mundane from the dangerous. I know what a potential mugger looks like, but I also know what a SoHo poseur looks like, and I can tell them apart. Here, anyone on the street could have been Jack the Ripper or Santa Claus. I didn't know enough about Baltimore, or Baltimore style, to tell. Now that Jon was ranting again, he was getting his audience back. We kept collecting little knots of middle-aged ladies with hard-leather pocketbooks and men in uniform overalls and rain gear. In New York, we would also have collected a running commentary. People were more polite here. The only thing I heard, the whole time I stood there, was a soft feminine voice saying, "Dear, dear. He's going to catch such an awful cold."

I also heard Jon. He was much angrier at me than he had been at the cops, maybe because he knew me. I suppose he might have thought I owed him acquiescence—what he would have called "understanding." People make that switch so often, I've ceased to complain about it. Whatever his reasoning, he had kicked his voice box into high and was letting me have it. I could hear him so clearly, I thought the wind had died down. Then I saw the way it was pulling against his hair and realized it had actually gotten worse. So had the thunder. Yesterday, slipping and falling on sidewalks painted with ice, I had wished for warmer temperatures. I had gotten them. I was standing in the middle of one of the great electrical storms of all time.

"Jonathon," I said, "you're going to kill us standing here. Let's get out of the storm."

He seemed not to have heard me. After my first annoyance passed, I conceded he might not have. I have dealt with a number of crazies in my time—real ones, and the temporary kind concocted by stress and circumstance. When I talk to them, I almost instinctually modulate my voice and slow the meter of my speech. I think it has a soothing effect, which it might. The only effect it had here was to make me inaudible. Couples halfway up the block who only wanted to discuss bus schedules were shouting at each other.

I grabbed Jon's arm, tried dragging him again, and got nowhere. In the interests of not getting a serious respiratory disease, I turned around and tried dragging him in the opposite direction, toward the garage. This time, he came, although slowly. He had reached that point where what happened mattered less to him than who initiated the happening. He wanted to get onto the crime scene, but he didn't want me to be the one who got him there.

I dragged him up to the entrance ramp, shrugged at the two cops in the cruiser and pushed Jon so that he stumbled just under the concrete portico. Then I marched past him, up the incline, until I was entirely out of the rain. He might be willing to risk a hospital stay to prove how iron-willed he was. I was not.

"For Christ's sake," I said. "I don't blame them for treating you like a crazy. You're acting like one. I gave you some sensible advice. If you didn't want to take it, all you had to do was say so. My nephews had more sense when they were going through the terrible twos."

"You were pushing me," he said.

"I took your arm," I corrected. "It's a common practice of courtesy. I won't do it again."

"People are always pushing me," he said. "Pushing me or trying to trick me. People are always—" He looked down at his hand. The dye in his coat was running, sending a rivulet of gray down the length of his fingers. He must have been out there getting wet for even longer than I realized. A coat that expensive would take a lot of abuse before it ran. "Shit," he said.

"You've only got yourself to blame," I said.

"I want to go up there and see her," he said. "I want to talk to the police. I want to know what's going on. It's *important* to me."

"Evelyn was important to you," I said. "I know."

*"Everybody* tries something," he said. "People think I'm a wimp. I'm not a wimp."

"I never said you were."

"We were out all afternoon yesterday," he said. "I told you about that. She knew the city really well. And then when I got back to the hotel, I came up to see you, and since then— She died before the party, didn't she? If she hadn't been dead she would have come. Evelyn always did her work."

"They won't know that until they've done what they have to do," I said, "but you're probably right. What time did you get back to the hotel?"

"Yesterday? About three. I came right up to see you. To see Phoebe, I mean. I like Phoebe."

"Everybody likes Phoebe."

"I don't think everybody likes anyone. Some people don't like anybody at all."

I pointed up to the garage. "Are you going to be any help in there? Do you know anything? Do you know what Evelyn was going to do after she left you?"

"What she was going to do? She had to go over to the store. To put books out, you know. And then she was supposed to come back to her room and get dressed. She'd bought a new dress for the party. That wasn't like her. She almost never bought clothes. Maybe she thought it was the last party on the tour and everything—"

"Mmm," I said.

"You never understood Evelyn," he said. "Nobody ever understood Evelyn."

I said "Mmm" again and backed up a little. At the far end of the room, the lab boys were packing up. The arc lamps had been taken down and folded up and tucked into nylon bags. Barbara Defborn was standing near the garage's office door, talking to an agitated Tempesta Stewart. There was no sign of Evelyn's body. I tried to remember if I'd heard anything that might have been the coroner's wagon arriving or leaving—it was the kind of thing I could have missed during the fuss out there—but came up blank. The garage no longer looked like a crime scene. What it did look like was a location shot for *Hill Street Blues*. Sitting in the middle of it, looking for an excuse to get out, I'd been *aware* of the dirt. Now I was assaulted by it. Everything in the place was covered by a thin film of grease, and all the grease looked lumpy.

I backed up a little. "Barbara's probably coming right over to the hotel," I told Jon. "She'd have gone to your room first thing. She *wants* to talk to you, for God's sake. You could have asked her anything you wanted then."

"I'm going to ask her anything I want to now. Get out of here, Patience."

"Right," I said.

He turned his deep brown eyes on me. "It's all your fault, you know. You and all the rest of them. You people ask for things like this."

"What?"

"She told me all about you. All about all of you. It's all your fault."

He turned around and started to walk away from me, toward a very surprised Barbara Defborn and a Tempesta Stewart who looked ready to kill him.

I went back to the hotel, but beyond that I showed no common sense at all. I should have gone straight up to my room and changed my clothes. Even if I was willing to stay wet for a while, I should have gone in search of Nick and Adrienne and Phoebe. The cops have the perfect excuse for dropping everything and running off to investigate a crime. They get paid for it. I have responsibilities.

This time, at least, I wasn't dumping my responsibilities out of sheer curiosity. I was boiling. On the walk back to the hotel, I kept thinking about Jon Lowry and the scene on the street, and the more I thought the more I came up with a scenario I didn't like. Christopher Brand had told Jon Lowry that Evelyn was dead. I could almost hear him doing it, choosing his words with all the care he would have needed if he'd wanted to be kind—except that he wouldn't have wanted to be kind. He'd have wanted to score. Christopher always wanted to score. He wanted to score with women. He wanted to score with books. He wanted to score with arguments. He could turn a conversation about the weather into a contest.

The state Jon had been in in front of the garage was not natural to him—or at least not natural to him as he had been since I'd known him. That wasn't very long, but the circumstances were unusual. We'd been living in close proximity for weeks. Surely, if he was prone to this kind of thing, I'd have seen it before.

I ducked under the hotel canopy, pushed through the great double doors and shook myself out on the carpet. I felt claustrophobic almost immediately. Staying in hotels always does this to me, no matter how good the hotel or how large the rooms or how pleasant the staff. I always feel confined, and after a while I'm willing to do anything to get out into an unfamiliar space.

The claustrophobia slowed me up a little. I looked toward the reception desk. The clerk there was young and perky and very professional, more like a high-powered secretary than a receptionist. She was not, however, anybody I remembered seeing before. She stood in front of her computer terminal in a uniformlike suit, tapping away at a keyboard while she kept a smile plastered to her face. The man in front of her looked almost as bedraggled as I knew I did. He had a brown fabric suitcase that seemed to have soaked through.

I turned away from them and headed for the elevator bank. The little hall in front of it was full of people. A gaggle of what seemed to be schoolteachers stood off to one side, rehashing a trip to some monument somewhere and worrying about their slides.

"It's the light," one of them kept saying. "My slides always come out all right if I've got enough real light, but when I have to work the light out for myself, you know, with bulbs—"

"I can't believe you haven't figured out how to work an automatic flash," another one said. "After all this time. They wouldn't let us out of college without knowing how to do that. Of course, that was when teachers college meant something. That's when we called a teachers college a teachers college. What's going on now—"

"They wanted to give one of those competency tests but they had to back off. They gave it the first time and a third of the teachers in the system didn't pass . . ."

I went to the wall and pushed the up button, mostly to give myself something to do. It was already lit.

I stepped back into the crowd—well back, so no one would think I was trying to jump them and force my way onto an elevator I hadn't paid my waiting dues to get. As I did, I bumped into somebody's suitcase, the hard-edged kind with sharp corners. I felt the scrape of metal against the denim of my jeans and then the sting of a twisted thread of it going right through to my skin. I jerked forward, clamping my teeth down so my *ouch* wouldn't be too loud. Suitcases with that kind of frame always end up spouting metal threads like porcupine quills. It wasn't anyone's fault, and I was in no mood to be apologized to.

The moving hadn't helped. The metal was still sticking into me. I twisted, looked down the length of my leg and saw that my jeans were caught on the corner of a square, hard-sided synthetic-shell case, bright red. The woman it belonged to had put it on the floor and taken her hand off it. She was indicating ownership by keeping one nylon-covered leg against the side. Late twenties, mousy brown hair in one of those California cuts, rigid set to the lips. She might or might not have belonged to the schoolteachers' tour, or whatever it was, but she was definitely not someone I wanted to know. Or get an apology from. I bent over and started to work the denim free with my left hand.

It is one of the great inconveniences of my life that I am about as far from ambidextrous as I can get. My left hand might as well be inoperative. I can't do much with it beyond propping things up and pushing open swing doors. The metal thread was thin and crooked and firmly embedded in the fabric of my jeans. My fingers fumbled against it without doing any good. I stood upright again. The man on the other side of the woman with the suitcase caught my eye and smiled.

"Help you?" he said.

"Can't," I said.

He looked at our mutual problem and shrugged. I decided I liked him. He was very young and looked uncomfortable in his suit. Very young men ought to look uncomfortable in suits.

The elevators were taking forever to get to the lobby. A woman at the front was poking at the up button again and again and again. On some older elevators, doing that will make a bell ring in the cab. Whether the newer variety did that or not, I didn't know. I was hoping it didn't. The crowd had been thick enough when I first arrived. Since then, there had been a veritable population explosion. The utility hall was very wide, but not wide enough to accommodate all this. I had been wedged in. In the hope that I'd been mistaken about the woman with the suitcase—I had Margaret Keeley on the brain; maybe I just thought this stranger was the same type—I looked back and reassessed. There was nothing to reassess. She was positively scary.

The young man tapped me on the shoulder and cleared his throat. "Excuse me," he said. "Are you all right?"

"I'm stuck on this woman's suitcase," I said.

"I know that." There was a grinding in the elevator shaft and we all looked expectant. Nothing happened.

"Why I want to know if you're all right," he said, "is that you seem to have injured your hand."

I looked down at my left hand. That was the one I'd been using to try to extricate myself from the suitcase, and it was also the one closer to the young man. It looked all right to me. My clear nail polish was chipped—something only I would have noticed—and my knuckles were still beaded with rain, but there was nothing I would have described as "looking injured."

"It seems to be all right," I said.

"Not that one," he said. "The other one. I thought that might be why you weren't using both hands. Because your right one was injured. And if it was, you see, I thought of a way to deal with *this,* you know, that wouldn't get you into a lot of hassle."

Against the wall, a light went on over one of the elevators and a pinging noise announced it was about to open its doors. Pavlov-like, the whole crowd of us looked up to watch it happen. The woman whose suitcase I was stuck on moved forward aggressively, apparently oblivious to anything but her need to get to her room at the soonest possible moment. I didn't believe it. I was sure she'd been listening to everything the young man and I had said, and just didn't give a damn.

I looked down at my right hand. More chipped nail polish, more beads of rain. I twisted my wrist back and forth, trying to get a look at it in every possible angle of light. And then I caught it.

It ran across the soft web of skin between thumb and forefinger, in a curving line that was blurred at the edges, like frostbite that had started to spread. If I hadn't been dirty as well as wet, I'd have seen it right away. In certain kinds of light, it bled into the grease I'd picked up in the garage.

A streak of blue wash, like ink.

"Oh hell," I said.

"Pay?" Phoebe said. "I've been looking all over for you."

*"Are* you all right?" the young man said.

"I'm fine."

In front of me, the woman with the hard suitcase grabbed its handle and charged for the open elevator doors. As she did, she tore a hole in my jeans from the top of my calf to my ankle.

# SIXTEEN

Phoebe didn't want to let me change my clothes. It was so out of character, I chalked it up to pregnancy. I was sopping wet, and she must have realized I hadn't had a thing to eat. Food, clothing and shelter have always been Phoebe's priorities. In the face of imminent nuclear war, she would stop peace negotiations to determine whether everyone at the bargaining table had had enough breakfast. Now she trailed me up to our floor, protesting all the way.

"You don't understand," she kept saying. "Hazel said it was urgent. Really urgent. Send out the alarms."

I unlocked the door to what had been our room, gave my hand another look and headed for the luggage. Phoebe's luggage was still all over the place. There was no sign of Nick. Or Adrienne.

"I'm not going anywhere like this," I said. "I look drowned and I'm torn. That woman. What's this stuff on my hands?"

"You keep asking me that."

"I know I keep asking you that. I want to know. It was on Margaret Keeley's face when we found her body. It was on Evelyn's."

"Maybe it's some kind of mark," Phoebe said. "Like death in that story on *The Twilight Zone*. Just before the people would die, they'd get a mark—"

"Thanks a lot, Phoebe."

"You shouldn't be so concerned with fashion," Phoebe said. "Nobody will notice where we're going anyway. Hazel said she was down at an Ad Hoc center."

"I'm just getting into a new pair of jeans."

Actually, I was getting into a new pair of jeans, a new shirt and another of Nick's sweaters. I'd bought him the one I'd been wearing, and it was ruined. I took it off and threw it in the bathtub, so it wouldn't do anything permanent to the hotel's bedspreads. Then I started searching for clean underwear.

"What's Hazel in such a panic about anyway?" I said. "And what's she doing at an Ad Hoc center? I didn't even know they had an Ad Hoc center in Baltimore."

"I didn't either. I thought the only one was in New York. And I don't know what she's in such a panic about. I just know she's in a panic. And—"

"Yes?"

"Well. It has something to do with Christopher Brand."

I put down the shirt I'd been considering. "Christopher Brand?"

"Nick said to tell you he talked to his friend at the IRS. He said he'd know what it was all about by this afternoon."

Phoebe does this sort of thing all the time. As usual, I was left gasping for context. I ran it through my head once or twice and then remembered the penultimate kicker on the phone when Nick had arrived the day before. The last thing he'd told me was that David was missing. The second-to-the-last was that I'd had some kind of letter from the IRS. I dumped this where it belonged, meaning right out of my head. Writers are always getting letters from the IRS, because the IRS always thinks we're cheating. Most of us aren't, but most of us are doing something the IRS thinks is just as bad—not understanding our tax forms. This should come as no surprise to anyone. Even the IRS doesn't understand the tax forms, and the rules they apply to writers have all been formulated for other kinds of businesses, most of which operate nothing at all the way writers do. Add to that the simple fact that the IRS doesn't have to worry about the Constitution at all—Jon Lowry was right about that—and trouble is practically inevitable. I'd spent nearly two solid weeks with my accountant trying to figure out how to deduct business expenses the way these people wanted me to under the new act, and neither he nor I had any idea if we'd done it right. It had gotten to the point where I didn't worry about it. The government had decided it had more right to the money I worked for than I did. It had also decided that it could spend that money any way it wanted to, and I had no right to complain in any effective way. If I spent any time thinking about this stuff, I started wanting to emigrate to Switzerland. I hate Switzerland. If I'd inadvertently messed up my forms, the IRS would send me a bill.

I found an oxford button-down I must have had since I was at Emma Willard and put it on.

"Forget my taxes," I said. "Talking about my taxes gets me agitated. Are you sure you don't know what that blue stuff is?"

"I'm sure. And I don't know what Hazel wants, but we'd better go. She really was frantic, Patience."

"Okay." My clean jeans were in my suit carrier, on a hanger. God only knew why. "What about Adrienne?" I asked.

"She's out at lunch with Nick," Phoebe said. "I was going to give her lunch in the hotel, but he knew a place on the harbor, and I was feeling sick again. When they're done, he's going to call New York and see if there's been any word about David at the office."

"Do you want him to find David?"

"I don't know."

"That's what I've liked best about this trip," I said. "Everybody's been so damn decisive."

I grabbed a folding traveling umbrella from one of Phoebe's open trunks and headed for the door.

Half an hour later, the cab I'd managed to find after another good dousing pulled up at the address Hazel Ganz had given Phoebe, and all I could think of was that if this was the Ad Hoc office in Baltimore —or anywhere else—then the Ad Hoc was in a lot of trouble. Every city has sections its Chamber of Commerce would prefer visitors not to see, and this was definitely Baltimore's. The street was full of potholes. At least half the streetlamps seemed to have had their glass fixtures cracked by flying rocks. Most of the buildings on the block looked like they'd been built for some kind of industrial use, but not inhabited for years. They were all cement-block and factory-plant brick, dinosaurs of the Industrial Revolution.

I looked quizzically at Phoebe. She checked her three-by-five card and nodded. I shrugged and climbed out onto the pavement.

The ride over had been silent and mostly unenlightening. Phoebe was feeling sick again. I couldn't think of a thing to ask her. Now, of course, I could think of a hundred things I should have. Like why the Ad Hoc Committee for Advocacy for the Homeless would *have* a Baltimore office. Why not do what they said they did almost every place else but in New York, where the national headquarters were—meaning operate out of people's living rooms?

At least the rain had eased off. I drew in close to no. 1464 to get out of the wind, and waited for Phoebe to catch up to me.

"Well," she said, "it makes sense. I mean, you wouldn't have an organization for the homeless on Park Avenue, would you?"

"Does Baltimore have a Park Avenue? Is it a good address?"

"Don't quibble, Patience." She walked up to the door and stood on tiptoe to get a peek through the small window at the top. The window was double-paned and wired, the way the windows in fire doors and buildings in high crime areas always are. I wasn't sure if this was a high crime area or not. It looked like it ought to be, except there wasn't anybody around to play criminal *or* victim.

Phoebe stepped away from the door. "Maybe there's a buzzer. That's a hall in there."

"You're absolutely sure this is the right address?" I asked her.

Phoebe snorted. "I know I'm a little distracted these days, Patience. I had her repeat it twice. Then I wrote it down. Then I read it back to her. This is the address."

"And she didn't say what it was about?"

"She called Christopher Brand a son of a—"

"Never mind."

"She called him that six times, Patience."

I checked the door, but there was no buzzer. I pulled on it, just in case I'd been wrong in assuming it was locked. It wouldn't budge. I walked to the left and tried to get a peek through the window, but I had no joy there either. That window was also double-glassed and wired, but at some time in the past it had been breached. Its surface boasted a spiderweb of cracks in one corner and two holes the size of fists in another. It had been backed with a piece of warped and discolored plywood.

"Nothing?" Phoebe said.

"The place looks entirely uninhabited," I said. "And it doesn't look too safe. God, if Evelyn was going to have a Baltimore office, she could have done better than this."

"Maybe they're upstairs."

Phoebe backed up, all the way to the end of the pavement. Like the street, the sidewalk had been almost viciously neglected. It was full of holes, and its edge was uneven, as if it had settled into soft ground.

Phoebe tottered a little, looked down at the mess she was in and then stepped onto the asphalt. There wasn't any traffic in sight.

She shielded her eyes with one hand and gazed upward. "Patience?" she said. "Maybe you should come look at this."

"What?"

"Third floor."

I went to stand beside her, and immediately found out why she'd shielded her eyes. There was no sun, but there was still a lot of rain. Without my hand to protect them, my eyes kept filling up with water. I made like an Indian scout and squinted at the windows on the third floor.

My height gave me an advantage. What Phoebe had probably seen was Christopher Brand's body, seeming to float by itself in the air. What I saw was not only the body but the two women carrying it. They were staggering.

"My God," I said.

"Is he dead?" Phoebe said. "He looks discorporeal."

"I don't know."

I leaned over, got a piece of indefinable rubble from the street and chucked it upward. I missed. I got another and tried again. This time, I must have hit something, although I didn't see it happen. The two women stopped struggling and turned toward the window. I got a third piece of rubble and tried again.

"This is weird," I said. "You know what I was doing when you found me? I was on my way to Christopher Brand's room."

"Wet like that?"

"Here they come."

Actually, only one of them was coming, but that was enough. Hazel Ganz had her hands around Christopher's feet. She didn't let go. She just swung herself around and drew closer to the window, looking down.

A second later, she dropped the feet, rushed to the window and threw it open.

"Thank God," she said. "We've been going crazy. Come to the door and I'll buzz you in."

"Hazel," somebody said from behind her. "You let go of him. He fell on me."

The hallway was a long, narrow space with graffiti on the walls, proof positive that life had existed in this part of town once upon a time. It wasn't mindless graffiti either. There were no Anglo-Saxon declarations of what the reader could do with himself. There were no monuments to Luis 25 or Harold 169. There were pictures, in spray-paint primary colors, of dragons and knights and damsels in mantillas.

I locked the door behind us as soon as we were inside, just in case the neighborhood was not as deserted as it appeared. There was a single bulb in the hall ceiling, not much help but better than total darkness. There was a door that must have led to the room the ground-floor window had been for. It was boarded over with strips of plywood and had a sign on it that said KEEP OUT.

I moved to the back and found a set of metal garbage cans, empty, and a fire door with BASEMENT stenciled on it. I turned back to Phoebe and shrugged.

"There has to be a way up," I said. "I just can't find it."

"Patience?" Hazel Ganz's voice floated at me out of the gloom. "Over here."

I looked around, confused. There really didn't seem to be anything else back there. Garbage cans, basement door, pile of plywood sticks like the ones that had been nailed to the door in front. I gave the plywood sticks another examination.

"Patience," Hazel said again. "It's right there. Behind all that junk. There used to be a door but it was stolen."

"Don't shout," I called up to her. "When you shout, you echo."

"Sorry."

She'd shouted anyway. I went to the plywood sticks and picked through them. They were piled up so thickly, it was hard to understand how anyone had got past them, but that they could be gotten past, and that there was something to get to once you did, was becoming clear. On the wall behind there was a hole, not door-shaped but ragged. If all that had happened here was that someone had stolen a door, he must have tried to take the rest of the wall along with him.

I shoved plywood aside with my feet and clambered through. I found myself at the bottom of a flight of thick, narrow stairs, painted red. There was no light in the stairwell. The stairs might have gone up forever or stopped three steps above the last one I could see.

"Find it?" Hazel called down.

"Yes," I said. "Just a minute." I stuck my head back into the hall and waved at Phoebe. "Come on," I said. "I'll help you through."

"Are those stairs?" Phoebe asked.

"You got it."

She started slowly toward me, and I ducked back into the stairwell.

"You've got to be nuts," I said. "You must know she's pregnant. You must have realized she'd come with me if you left the message with her. What's gotten into you anyway?"

"Patience," Hazel said. "We've got an emergency here."

"Is he dead?"

"Dead drunk, maybe."

That was a relief. I heard the sound of plywood falling and darted back into the doorway to help Phoebe through. She looked like she was about to be sick again, and I didn't blame her. There was an underlying smell to the place that got to you after a while. It was sweet and wet, like organic maple syrup gone to mold. I put my hand out and let Phoebe use it for a cane. She slid a little, but she made it.

"What's going *on* here?" she said.

"According to Hazel, Christopher Brand is drunk."

"So what else is new?" Phoebe said. "She got us all the way out to this place because of that? He gets drunk all the time. And ends up in the tank. And comes out looking like a bum and talking like a martyr."

"Why don't we just go up and see," I said.

Phoebe grunted. "There isn't any light. I don't even know if I can fit up those things."

There was a rustling at the top and a nasal hum that might have been two voices whispering. Then there was a groan, and Hazel said, "He's waking up. Oh, dear God in heaven, don't let him wake up."

I climbed two steps. "Hazel?"

"Get up here fast," Hazel shouted. "I'm not kidding, Patience. I'm desperate."

"Hazel, what are you doing here? What's Christopher doing here? What am *I* doing here?"

"You're here because I called you," Hazel snapped. "And I'm here because *he* called *me*. What the hell do you *think?*"

"Why would Christopher Brand call you?"

Another groan. Another spate of panicked whispering. Something that sounded like a foot coming in contact with a door.

"Oh, for God's sake," Hazel said. "Why did he call me? Why do you think he called me? Because I've been sleeping with him since Minneapolis, that's why he called me. Will you two please get *up* here?"

She was shouting again. Her nasal Midwestern twang bounced down the stairwell like an accusation made on a xylophone.

# SEVENTEEN

The upstairs room was in much better shape than what we'd seen of the rest of the building—but that wasn't saying much. It must have been a dance studio once. The exercise bars were still up on the north wall, and the south wall was solid with mirrors. The rest of the room was given over to a more recent purpose. Stacks of pamphlets and newsletters were everywhere, their banners spelling out THE PEOPLE'S CENTER FOR SOCIAL ACTION in hand-drawn letters. File folders were piled into torn cardboard boxes, some marked in red with KEEP and others in blue with DUMP. There had to be twenty-five or thirty telephone jacks under the line of windows that faced the street. The phones were gone, but when they'd been in the place must have done record Ma Bell business.

I pushed Phoebe into the room's only chair and looked down at Christopher Brand, lying at the feet of a woman who looked both exasperated and indignant. She was dressed in the uniform of Young People with a Social Conscience everywhere, right down to the earth shoes and the white socks with the yellow stripe on the cuffs. Her hair was long and colorless and pulled away from her face with a rubber band at the nape of her neck. She had a nail-biting habit even worse than mine.

I shot Hazel an inquiring glance. Hazel shrugged.

"This is Darcy Penter," she said. "She runs this place."

"I don't run this place," Darcy said waspishly. "I'm just organizing our move. Or I was, until *he* showed up."

"You've found new quarters?" It was a silly thing to say. I wished I hadn't.

Darcy, fortunately for me, was glad I had. "You can't begin to understand how hard it is," she said. "Things change so fast. I never knew that until I started working here. None of us did. We thought we'd go into a bad neighborhood and try to make it better. And we did. But the neighborhoods—the first place we had, the block went yuppie just like that. In less than a year. And now *this.*"

"It does look abandoned," I said.

"It might as well be the Sahara Desert," Darcy said. "Our entire constituency just packed up and moved out. They didn't even move any place we could follow them. Some corporation came and bought up all the property around here, and the city made them pay to move people, and the people all wanted to go to . . . Well, we couldn't follow them."

"Could we get to the point here?" Hazel said. *"Him."*

We all turned to stare at Christopher once again. He was snoring noisily into the hardwood, looking peaceful.

"I can't tell you anything about him," Darcy said. "He just came bombing up here about an hour and a half ago, asking all kinds of questions, and then he ran off somewhere and must have used the phone. And had about six drinks. The next thing I know, he's passed out cold and she's on the doorstep, wanting to know what's going on."

"Did he tell you what he came for?"

Darcy sighed. "He said it was about that Housing Project thing. The Ad Hoc Committee for Advocacy for the Homeless. But I couldn't tell him anything. I mean, we did try to do something with that. We're very concerned about the homeless. We sent away for their literature and we tried to do an education campaign, but they were just so disorganized. We'd ask for material and never get it. Or we'd call and try to talk to somebody about getting speakers or slide shows and we'd never find anybody who knew what was going on. By that time we'd listed them as one of our contact organizations, so when the tour came everybody thought we knew something, but we didn't. We didn't even want to."

"He said on the phone that he had it all figured out," Hazel said. "He was really ranting, Patience, I'm not kidding. Laughing his head off. He must have been drunk even then."

"And you came right out to rescue him," I said.

Hazel flushed. "Don't make me sound like a ninny. I'm not. I'd have come out for anybody I knew. And this did sound strange."

"Why? As far as I can tell, it's just the sort of thing you'd expect from something Evelyn was involved in. None of her organizations was effective. None of them was efficient. Hell, if it ran well, she didn't want to know about it."

"But Evelyn's missing," Hazel pointed out. "And that woman is dead. So if there was a scam at The Housing Project—"

Phoebe and I exchanged a look. Hers had a smile attached to it, but not a very nice smile. I got out my cigarettes, friends in need and refuge of first resort whenever I'm under stress.

"Hazel," I said, "Evelyn isn't missing."

"She's come back?"

"Why do I always get involved in these things?" Phoebe said. "Why me?"

Phoebe got involved in these things because she asked to come along, but she knew that. I got my lighter out and lit up.

"Evelyn's dead," I said. "We found her body in the trunk of Tempesta Stewart's car just a little while ago. It looks like the same kind of thing that happened to Mrs. Keeley."

Death had an effect on Darcy Penter that nothing else could have, not even a declaration of solidarity for the people's struggle for whatever. Whether it was curiosity or sympathy wasn't clear, but what it resulted in was instant coffee out of a thermos and a glass of Poland Springs water for Phoebe. In no time at all, we were sitting on the floor in a politically correct circle, behaving as if we were out to lunch with our mothers.

"I'm really not the kind of fool you think I am," Hazel said. "I know what he is. I knew it from the beginning. That was the point."

"Letting him jump your bones and insult you at the same time was the point?" I said.

"You're not being fair," Phoebe said.

"Sex was the point," Hazel said. "Oh, for God's sake. You know how long I've been divorced? Seven years. You know how many affairs I've had in all that time? Two. Both at conferences. I don't want to pull that kind of thing at home with the children around to watch me, and I don't want to do it where my ex-husband can hear about it either. He's been pushing the custody thing since the day I walked out on him. He started out saying I'd never be able to support them all, but romance took care of that. With sex—"

"Cleveland is Cleveland," Phoebe said solemnly.

"Cleveland is not the back of beyond," Hazel said tartly. "Oh, who am I kidding? I don't know what Cleveland's like with that kind of thing. I've never had to face it. And I never intend to. So—"

"So you got horny and Christopher was available," I said.

"Actually, it was Christopher who got horny and I who was available, but I wish you wouldn't put it like that. Oh hell. Why not?"

"It just makes me crazy," I said. "You're an intelligent woman. You should know better."

"Know better than what? I sure as hell know better than to think Prince Charming is going to come along. Why do you think my books don't sell better than they do? I'm always putting in things about not trusting to true love and God knows what else. But anyway, it wasn't just the sex. I was beginning to think of him as an interesting psychological type."

"That's one way of putting it," I said.

"No, really," Hazel insisted. "He changed after Minneapolis. He really did. Not from sleeping with me. Or not *about* sleeping with me, at any rate. He—before then, he was all bravado. He'd talk about how he didn't have to give a shit about anything, not any of the rest of us on the tour or Evelyn or Jon Lowry's money or the booksellers. But he didn't mean it. He was scared to death. It'd been years since he'd been on the tour circuit. Nobody wanted him. Nobody trusted him. His publishers were keeping it quiet, but it was really affecting his sales. His last two books made the best-seller lists only because they were released into dead time. In the beginning, he could get right on there with Stephen King and Jean Auel as competition."

"And he lost his bravado after Minneapolis?" I said.

"He didn't lose it, exactly," Hazel said. "He lost the fake. He wasn't frightened anymore. It was like he had something new. Something he could count on."

"What?"

"I don't know." She frowned into her coffee, which was decaffeinated and filmy on top. "I can tell you when," she said. "Almost to the minute."

"When he changed?"

"Uh-huh. You remember when we had that cocktail party, the one the Minneapolis AWR gave?"

"We ought to," Phoebe said. "One of Tempesta's fans told Pay she was a tool of the devil and poured a pitcher full of punch down her dress."

"I think that woman had been smoking marijuana," I said.

"Never mind the woman," Hazel said. "The thing is, when we went into that, he was just the same. In fact, he was pushing. He used to do that. He'd get all insecure, and start ranting and railing about how Evelyn was using him, forcing him into things like the tour when she knew he was down, making him do stupid stuff that would embarrass him. That cocktail party really made him mad. He hates being around romance writers. He thinks it hurts his status. Anyway, we were there for about half an hour, and he got a phone call from his lawyer."

"How do you know it was from his lawyer?" I asked.

"He said so when he came back. The cocktail party was in the hotel, and they paged him and he went to the phone. When he came back, he was as high as Lydia gets when she takes those pills. And that's not all."

"Christ, you'd think it would be enough," I said. "Why is it that with Christopher nothing is ever 'all'?"

"Mid-life crisis," Hazel said dismissively. "The thing is, he's really obsessive about sex. He wants it all the time. We'd started sleeping together about two days before the cocktail party, and we'd been at it every second we didn't have to appear in public. Then that night, all he wanted to do was talk on the phone. He must have called everybody he knew. His editor. His regular publicist. His accountant."

"I don't like the sound of that," Phoebe said. "Everything we've ever gotten mixed up in, it's had accountants in it somewhere."

"Yes, well. I thought he was just easing off—and thank God, quite frankly, because I really don't have that kind of drive. But the next day he was right back at it, just like nothing had happened. Except that he was—different."

I thought back. "You know," I said finally, "you're right. He didn't start to needle Jon Lowry until after Minneapolis. In Philadelphia and Boston he just stayed out of Jon's way."

"Oh, Jon Lowry," Hazel said. "He really hates Jon Lowry. I don't know what it is. Jealousy over the money, probably. And all that publicity without having to do anything for it. Chris told me once that Jon could get a book on the *Times* list any time he wanted to, just because people were impressed with billionaires. I was surprised when he started all that stuff, really. Calling Jon a wimp and telling him he'd make a great faggot and all the rest of it. Evelyn protected Jon like—well, all I can think of is clichés."

"Evelyn and Jon inspire clichés," I said.

"Did she really die just the way Mrs. Keeley did? With that puncture thing on the back of her neck?"

I nodded. "Barbara Defborn told me the examination of Mrs. Keeley showed an almost perfect puncture—some method they use to kill lab animals for dissection. Except that instead of using whatever it was they use for that—a thin wire thing, I forget what Barbara called it—"

"A sterile awl," Darcy Penter put in helpfully. She blushed. "I was very good in biology. Until I realized how scientists are inevitably co-opted by the military-industrial complex, I thought I might be one. You have to sterilize the awl because if you don't you end up with foreign bacteria in the tissues, and when you look through the microscope, you don't know what you're seeing."

"Thanks," I said. "Whoever it was didn't use one of those. Barbara says the coroner thinks the weapon was one of those big needles they use to inject doses of poison antidote in emergencies. They're about eight inches long and the needle is really thick. And hollow. She said that was a good thing and a bad thing, at least as far as killing was concerned. It was bad because the needle is almost too thick. The area of vulnerability back there isn't very large. It was a good thing because it not only managed to cause trauma going in, it sucked up necessary tissue going out. That way, if the killer didn't know what he was doing, he could still be fairly sure of causing permanent damage. He'd have taken out enough spinal fluid to cause paralysis and brain damage at the least."

"Jesus," Hazel said.

"It's even worse than that," I said. "They found Mrs. Keeley's blood loaded with Darvocet. He drugged her first so he could be sure she wouldn't move."

"He or she," Hazel said. "It could have been Tempesta Stewart."

I got to my feet. "It could have been *him,*" I said, pointing my toe at Christopher Brand. "You're the one who said he hated us."

"Why would he bother to kill Mrs. Keeley? And I didn't say he hated us. I said he hated Jon Lowry. I think he just thought the rest of us were monuments to the boob mentality of the American reading public. So to speak."

"I know another reason he might have used a needle like that instead of a sterile awl," Darcy Penter said.

We all turned to look at her and she flushed again, something that must have been a habit with her.

"The thing is," she said, "to get a sterile awl, you'd have to go to a scientific supply house, or a medical one. They don't sell sterile awls in your local K Mart. And the supply houses keep records of the equipment they sell, just in case there's an investigation into somebody's medical license or research or something."

"They sell these needle things at K Mart?"

"Not at K Mart, but at most pharmacies. Because of bee stings, you know."

"No," I said. "I don't know."

"People are allergic to bee stings," Darcy said. "And wasp stings, too. That's even more dangerous. And there are these kits you can buy, with the antidote in them, and they come with a plunger and a supply of those needles. They're bigger than the kind people use for insulin. With wasp stings especially, you have to get a lot of countermeasure into the system fast. People with allergies to them can die of wasp stings in thirty seconds."

"Wouldn't you need a prescription for one of those things?" I asked. "In New York, you have to have a prescription for any kind of hypodermic."

"I don't know," Darcy said.

"I'll bet you do," I said.

Phoebe sighed. "Here we are again. No way for the murderer to get the murder weapon without leaving a trail."

"Well, maybe he did leave a trail," Hazel said.

This time, it was her we all turned to see. She didn't flush. Hazel got embarrassed over revelations about her sex life, but she had long ago learned to stand up for her intelligence. Any romance writer who doesn't learn to do that early ends up convinced she's stupid.

"We've been talking and talking about all the cities we've been in," she said. "Why couldn't the murderer have decided on the killing back in Sherman Oaks or St. Louis or somewhere, and faked a prescription for this stuff and got it filled there, and then waited for here before killing anybody?"

"Before killing Mrs. Keeley?" I asked. "How could he know he'd want to? We didn't know Mrs. Keeley. Even Evelyn didn't meet her until we'd arrived. She's a friend of Gail Larson's."

"Who died first," Hazel said, "Mrs. Keeley or Evelyn?"

"They don't know," I said. "Circumstantial evidence suggests it was Evelyn."

"Well, then," Hazel said triumphantly. "So it was Evelyn who was supposed to die all along, and this Mrs. Keeley who got in the way. You're the one who writes about crime, Patience. You should know all this."

"Yes," I said, "but—"

"No buts. We really have to get Christopher out of here. He's due at an interview at four o'clock."

I had been due at an interview at two. I'd forgotten all about it.

# EIGHTEEN

Back in New York, I might have rushed right out and tried to get somebody to check prescriptions for bee-sting antidote. I would certainly have called Tony Marsh at Manhattan Homicide and demanded he look into it. I didn't have the kind of connections I needed in Baltimore. I promised myself I'd get in touch with Barbara Defborn as soon as I got back to the hotel, but that felt like a one-way street, away from me. I'd give her the information. I wasn't sure she'd give anything back.

In the meantime, Hazel and Phoebe and I had the job of getting Christopher Brand safely into a hotel bed. He was out cold and dead weight. I'd once carried Lydia Wentward halfway across Manhattan after she'd passed out in a bar in Times Square during the Third Annual Conference of the American Writers of Romance, but I'd had a flock of readily available cabs to help me and a body that weighed no more than one-ten. Christopher Brand weighed close to two hundred pounds. When we got him down to the street, it was obvious there wasn't a cab in the city of Baltimore that would come down that block unless it was radioed for. I looked around for the phone Christopher must have used to call Hazel and found nothing. The bar he'd had his drinks in wasn't visible either. God only knew how far he'd had to walk.

I'd had Hazel lay him down on the pavement while I searched in the distance for passing vehicles—any passing vehicles, including police cars. Now I walked back and stood over him. The project might have been remotely feasible if Phoebe were able to help, but she wasn't. Even if she offered—and she had sense enough not to—I wouldn't have let her try.

"We're going to have to think of something else," I said. "We'll never get him where we need him to go at this rate."

"We ought to hurry, too," Hazel said. "He does have that interview."

"He isn't going to make that interview," I said. "Even if we get him back in time, he isn't going to be awake."

"Yes, he is," Phoebe said.

She pointed at the sidewalk. We had laid him on his back, mostly because we'd been carrying him face up. The rain had stopped, but the gutters weren't dry. Neither were the roofs. Without realizing it, we'd put him down just under a spot where the wind was dumping spatterings of rain blown from the surfaces of the surrounding buildings. Under the periodic assaults of cold water, he had begun to stir.

Phoebe bent over and put her ear close to his mouth. "Water torture," she said. "He keeps saying 'water torture.' "

"I ought to set fire to his feet," I said. "Where's a puddle?"

"What's the matter with you?" Hazel said. "The street is full of puddles."

She was right. I walked out to the biggest pothole I could see. It was full of muddy, foul-looking water and the corpses of drowned bugs. I cupped my hands, stuck them in and brought out as much as I could. I didn't like it, but I knew I'd rather do it than spend the next four hours in this Godforsaken place waiting for him to wake naturally.

I walked back, stood over his head and let the water go. It splashed right into his eyes and ran down his cheeks. He jerked.

"You need more," Hazel said.

"You could go get some yourself."

Hazel sniffed. "*I'm* not the great detective. *I* don't have to subject myself to slime."

I walked back to the middle of the street, stuck my hands into the pothole again and came up with more "slime." It's remarkable how often I run into this attitude. People will say just about anything to justify not doing something they don't want to do. I walked the water back to Christopher and dumped it on his head again.

"What the f—"

"Get up," I said.

"Not quite," Phoebe said.

"Don't you believe it." I kicked against Christopher Brand's side, peremptorily. "I know you can open your eyes," I said, "so open them. Because if you don't, I'm going to get a load with pebbles in it next time."

"Shit," Christopher said.

"He talks in his sleep, but he doesn't swear when he does," I said. "I read it in the *National Enquirer.*"

"You believe the *National Enquirer?*" Hazel said.

"You *read* the *National Enquirer?*" Phoebe said.

"I do when I find it on the subway." I leaned over until I was right next to Christopher's ear. "Get up," I demanded. "We're in the middle of nowhere and I don't like this neighborhood. At least if you're on your feet, somebody may mistake you for a threat."

Christopher groaned, feebly and unconvincingly. Then he opened a single eye. "What?" he said.

I'd had it. I really had had it. I have put up with nonsense from men all my life. Every woman has. Colds played out with more panic and trauma than the Lady of the Camellias had managed to whip up for terminal-stage tuberculosis. Minor muscle strains parlayed into near paralysis. Cut fingers advanced to the status of mortal wounds. I'd seen every kind of male sickbed fakery devised. Even Nick indulged in it. I should have known.

"You should never have stopped snoring," I said. "It was a dead giveaway."

"Now, Patience," Christopher said. His voice was thick, but it was drunkenness, not leftover sleep.

"How long did you think you were going to keep this up?" I said.

"Keep what up?" Hazel said.

"You made Pay put her hands in that filth," Phoebe said. "How *could* you?"

"You mean he wasn't really passed out?" Hazel said.

"Oh, he was really passed out," I said. "That was real snoring I heard when I first came upstairs. I figure he woke up right around the time we started talking about Evelyn's murder. And he wanted to know what we had. And he was afraid he'd never get it. So—"

"You mean we carried him all the way down here when he could have walked himself?" Hazel said.

"Now, Hazel." Christopher was beginning to look uneasy. "I know it may seem a little strange, but I was just trying to—"

Hazel marched out to the pothole, filled her rain hat full of water and came marching back. When she got to Christopher, she dumped the whole load in his face.

I would have applauded that action if it hadn't been for the fact that Christopher Brand found a way to use it, the way he found a way to use everything. We all wanted to go back to the hotel. Neither Phoebe nor I liked being in a part of the city we didn't know. Of course, we didn't really know any of Baltimore, but at least most of the rest of what we'd seen of it was inhabited, and had street signs. Hazel had the romance writer's obsessiveness about interviews and media contacts. It was beyond her comprehension that any writer anywhere would deliberately stand up an interviewer. On that, I had the advantage. I had met alcoholics before.

Alcoholics being what they are, Christopher was too much for us. He wanted to drink. He wanted to drink now. He wanted to drink in a place that made him comfortable, which didn't include the well-lit bistro run by the hotel or the hanging-fern places that lined the harbor. I knew what kind of place we were headed for. If he hadn't known things I wanted him to tell me, I'd have left him on his own. When Hazel realized I was going to let him drag us into some dive, she almost left us on our own.

"How can you pander to that?" she demanded. "He's not in his right mind, and he's a son of a—"

"Hazel, I think it's about time we let up on his poor mother. He's probably not her fault. Anyway, he just might tell us—"

"I've been trying to get him to tell me for two weeks," she said. "What do you take me for?"

The "what do you take me for?" was weaker than it might have been. Hazel knew herself well. She had been brought up to be a nice little girl. She had a tendency to be overly polite, and deferential in situations where she should have been anything but. Christopher Brand turned the corner at the end of the block—in the wrong direction, by the way—and she followed us following him.

He walked another two blocks, turned another corner and walked three blocks more. The uninhabited industrial wasteland fell behind us, and we moved into an area of small grocery stores and large pawnshops. Phoebe trotted along cheerfully. Walking was the one kind of exercise she liked, and she kept chirping about how her doctor had said it was good for her. I wasn't taken in. Phoebe grew up in one of the uglier sections of Union City, but it was a respectable ugly section.

Pawnshops were exotic to her. They were exotic to me, too, but I didn't have the same perspective.

The bar Christopher Brand turned into was called the Green Door. I had the terrible feeling that it had been named for the porno movie. Stuffily middle-class neighbors are likely to think of the ordinary corner country bar as a "real sleaze joint," but that's lack of experience. The Green Door was a real sleaze joint. It was dirtier than Tempesta's friend's garage, and it smelled worse.

Christopher swung inside without slowing down. Either his sinuses were blocked or he liked that kind of thing, probably the latter. Hazel hesitated on the sidewalk.

"Maybe we shouldn't go in there," she said. "I know what you're trying to do, but—"

"I have to go in there," I said. "The two of you can catch a cab back to the hotel if you want. There's probably a phone inside."

"We couldn't leave you here all by yourself." Phoebe was appalled. "What if something happened?"

The truth was, nothing was likely to happen. Patrons of places like the Green Door are usually too whacked to start fights. This was the last stop before a paper bag and a bed made of park bench. I looked down at Phoebe's stomach.

"Go," I said.

"Come back with us," Phoebe said. "You can talk to him later."

"He's an alcoholic at the beginning of a binge, Phoebe. There's no telling when he'll be coherent again. The kind of thing you're worried about is no problem. The kind of thing I am might be. There are germs in there."

"You mean the baby," Phoebe said.

"Exactly."

"I'll take her back." Hazel grabbed Phoebe's arm and pulled her into the street, unwilling to go through that door even to call for help. If my sense of direction was right, they wouldn't have too far to walk. This was a bad block, but not as bad as the one we'd come from. The next one up would be better still. There would be working phone booths and little diners. They'd be fine.

I watched them until they disappeared.

Even if I'd had a taste for sleaze bars, I could never have become a habitué. I don't have the looks for it, and I don't move right. In low-life bars I tend to attract a lot of attention and a certain amount of hostility. It was a measure of just how low the life at the Green Door was that this time I attracted neither. In fact, I barely generated polite interest. I came in. I looked around until I found Christopher at the bar with a string of shot glasses in front of him. A couple of the patrons at the tables looked up and looked away again, registering nothing. The bartender paid no attention to me at all.

I crossed the room and climbed the stool next to Christopher's. The Green Door was the original no-frills bar: no television, no jukebox, no video games. The bar itself was wood only in the realm of imagination. It was made of cheap, hard plastic colored to look like grain.

Christopher drained one of his shot glasses and put it down in front of me. "You really came in here," he said. "I didn't think I was going to have to worry about that."

"I sent Hazel and Phoebe home."

"Hazel wouldn't have walked through that door if she thought this place was full of money. You going to order a drink?"

"No."

"I never knew you were a prude, Patience."

"I'm not a prude. I wouldn't want to put my mouth on one of the glasses."

"Patience, Patience, Patience. So genteel."

"Look," I said. "You may want to be in here, but I don't. All I want out of you are some answers. You pulled a very neat little trick back there. You got caught. You *owe* me."

"Do I?"

"I'm really not in any mood to put up with your crap."

He drained another of the shot glasses and stacked it into the one he'd drained before. His mood was hard for me to figure out—floaty, almost amused. He drained a third shot glass and stacked that one, too. Then he swiveled on his seat until he was facing me.

"Let me tell you what I think I owe you," he said. "Nothing. Absolutely nothing. You and all the rest of those people back there. None of you can write worth a damn. None of you would know sensibility if you were dying of it. None of you is anything but a machine for making money. Well, go back there and make it. I haven't had a serious drunk in six months."

"You've made twice the money I'll ever make from writing," I said, "and you know it."

"Oh, yeah. I've made money. And I've spent it. And I've bled for it, too. Prissy-faced little pains in the butt like Evelyn: Christopher, do this for me, Christopher, do that for me, Christopher, come on this tour. It will help you out. They'll take you back for charity. Charity. Bullshit."

*"Is* the Ad Hoc Committee a scam?"

He'd gone back to looking at shot glasses. This time, only his eyes turned toward me, sliding sideways in his face.

"Would you be surprised if I said it was?"

"I don't know. Evelyn was a flake and an enthusiast. I wouldn't be surprised if I heard she'd been taken for once. In a way, I'm surprised it hasn't happened before."

"That's what you think? Evelyn hasn't been taken before now?"

"Has she?"

"Let's get off Evelyn. Evelyn's dead."

"That's the point, Christopher."

"This is the point." He picked up another shot glass and held it up to the light. The liquid was too pale. The drinks were being watered in the bottle, half and half. "This is a scam," he said. "But at least it's a cheap scam. They charge a buck seventy-five. They give you a buck seventy-five worth of liquor, upscale prices. I just had one more thing I needed to put it together. I went up to that place, and there it was. Right out in front."

"How did you find out about that place?"

"It's on the program. You'd know that if you ever read the material Evelyn handed out. Not that anybody but me ever did. Anyway, it was sitting there at the end of the list of sponsoring organizations. 'Baltimore Office of the Ad Hoc Committee for Advocacy for the Homeless. Care of the People's Center for Social Action.' There was also an address. There was an address for the one in New Orleans, too, you know. I went there while the rest of you were doing the tour of Bourbon Street."

"Another office?" I was confused. "But with all those offices—

Christopher, what is this? A conspiracy theory? How could The Housing Project be a scam with all those people involved in it?"

"Your problem," Christopher said, "is that you absolutely refuse to accept the obvious."

He lunged at me, sticking his face so far forward, his nose touched mine. I'd never been afraid of him before. I had more sense than to be physically afraid of anyone that drunk. Still, he suddenly seemed dangerous in more ways than I wanted to count.

"Time," he said. "Time. None of you popular writers ever thinks enough about *time.*"

# NINETEEN

The first thing I intended to do after I got back to the hotel was call Barbara Defborn. Nick and Tempesta and I had all given her elaborate accounts of the notes, but I supposed she deserved to hear Christopher Brand's accusations, if accusations they were. The more I thought about it, the less sure I was. He'd certainly sounded as if he were saying that The Housing Project was a scam, and that made a kind of sense I liked. Charity scams are good ones—although they're best when they can be set up as a "religion." Religions not only don't have to pay taxes, they don't have to file. In fact, they don't have to account for their income anywhere, to anybody. Straightforward charity scams at least have to apply for tax-exempt status, which means somebody has to fill out a lot of forms for the government and keep a lot of records and hand all the numbers over once a year. On the other hand, numbers can be kited, books can be cooked and tax forms can be delayed with extensions. If the con didn't get too outrageous, or the conners too stupid, something like that could go on for a long time. While it lasted, it would bring in a lot of tax-free money.

I liked this scenario for other reasons, too. For one thing, it provided such a straightforward motive for murder. I didn't know how long The Housing Project had been in operation, but I was sure it hadn't been around long enough to attract the wrong kind of attention. If it was faked, there was still a lot of money to be made before whoever was doing the cheating needed to get nervous. The tour must have been bringing in a mint. I didn't know what we were making from the sale of books. I was usually signing in the back while that sort of thing was being handled at the front. I had, however, heard a lot about the take at the cocktail parties and the dinners—forty thousand from a "literary banquet" in New Orleans, twenty thousand for six hours of cocktails and book gossip in Boston, fifteen thousand for lunch in Philadelphia. Most charity functions had to worry about cost-price ratios, but the tour didn't. Jon Lowry was underwriting it. And Evelyn was good. She made the parties "selective" and "exclusive" and expensive as hell, drawing in the people who cared more about being important than they did about anything else. There are incredible numbers of people like that in the world. In a publishing-business town like New York, they know books and authors, even best-selling authors of Pulitzer Prize-winning books, can be had for no more trouble than it takes to make a phone call. In places like Jackson and Tampa, anything connected to anyone who appears regularly on Donahue and Carson has cachet. Evelyn knew what to do with that. Party followed party, each smaller and costlier than the last. A lists, B lists, C lists, Inner Circles: if Evelyn was coordinating society fund-raising for the Metropolitan Opera, they'd never have to worry about donations again.

Added to that, I had what I knew about Evelyn's character. Evelyn had never been able to transfer the insightfulness about human nature she brought to promotions to the charities she loved. If you could convince Evelyn you were working for some "victim" somewhere, she would follow you anywhere. I'd been serious when I told Christopher Brand that I'd be surprised if the Ad Hoc Committee was not only a scam but the first Evelyn had been taken in by. In a way, I thought she'd probably been taken in a hundred times before, although the people she'd been taken in by had probably been just as taken in themselves. People for Peace. Women for Social Equality. The Institute for Parental Control of the Schools. As far as I knew, all those organizations had been legitimate, they just hadn't *done* anything. Evelyn had a positive genius for finding ineffective groups with altruistic rationalizations for off-the-wall politics. She simply had no judgment when it came to social action.

What she did have was nearly limitless energy. Once Evelyn involved herself in a charitable enterprise, she gave everything she had to it, no matter how her work suffered. We'd complained about that for years. Tour schedules with holes in them big enough to drive a Sherman tank through. Interviewers who showed up frantic because the biographical material had never arrived. Dates and times transposed, so that at least once every tour you missed a connection or showed up at the wrong bookstore in the wrong city on the wrong night. A passion for charity was the single reason Evelyn hadn't gotten any further than she had at Austin, Stoddard and Trapp. She couldn't keep her mind off it long enough to get her mind on her work.

Even scam charities want willing workhorses, but I had a feeling no scam would welcome someone like Evelyn. Evelyn went in for total immersion. She got involved in everything, and she pushed. From what I could remember—I could have kicked myself for not having paid more attention to this at the time—she'd ended up heading at least one or two of the groups she'd gone to work for. The gay and lesbian groups had been beyond her grasp, but she'd been chairwoman of both People for Peace and the Institute for Parental Control of the Schools. I could just see her, oozing her way into every warp in the Ad Hoc Committee's fabric and coming up with—fraud.

Murder Evelyn because she discovered the fraud? Murder Margaret Johnson Keeley because—why? She saw you murder Evelyn? I didn't like that. I knew that sort of thing was done, in real life as well as in books, but this thing had been so well planned. Of course, that might be an illusion. The murder weapon might have been bought right here in Baltimore, at some perfectly ordinary pharmacy, and the evidence left lying around where Barbara Defborn could stumble across it in a day or two. I couldn't make myself believe it had happened that way. Even for a stupid murderer, or a frantic one, it would have been a hell of a risk. We'd had our pictures in the papers in every city we visited. In Baltimore, Evelyn had outdone herself. We'd been the subject of a media blitz. If the murderer bought that needle in Baltimore, all Barbara Defborn had to do was go on local television and ask about it. Everything from the phony prescription to an eyewitness would be sitting in her lap in a matter of hours. Unfortunately, I couldn't think of one damn reason for anybody to kill Margaret Keeley—except for Gail Larson. If I'd been Gail Larson, I'd have murdered the woman years ago.

The cab pulled up at the hotel and I got out, throwing a ten-dollar bill into the front seat. The weather had definitely improved. It was cold and getting colder, but the rain had stopped and no new nasty form of precipitation seemed about to arrive in its place. The unaccustomed meteorological calm did wonders for the Inner Harbor's Christmas decorations. It was five o'clock, already full dark, and the little display of twinkling lights on the tree in the lobby seemed perky and warm and cheerful. December 16. If Barbara Defborn did her job right, I'd be back in New York in a couple of days—and out in Connecticut a week after that. Once Adrienne and I had landed on my mother, I'd have the wedding preparations to deal with, but even my mother couldn't drive a person nuts twenty-four hours a day. (Was I sure?) I'd have hours and hours to spend at my two favorite activities: talking to Adrienne and reading really gory ghost stories under a quilt with a glass of Baileys Original Irish at my side. Fortunately, I had all my Christmas shopping done. The boxes were stashed in the hall closet of the apartment on Central Park West, beautifully wrapped. I'd had the department stores wrap them. When I wrap packages, they always end up with little horns of paper sticking out in unpredictable places. They look like Madonna's onstage hair.

I made my way into the lobby and toward the desk. If I'd gotten back earlier, I could have counted on Nick or Phoebe or Adrienne to be around to let me into some room someplace, but at this time of the afternoon, anything could be going on. Like most children, Adrienne got hungry early. The girls at Brearley had taught her it wasn't chic to eat before seven o'clock, or maybe eight, but she was always starving by five and ravenous by six. The girls at Brearley probably were, too. I'd go up and see if they were all waiting for me, but I wouldn't have my feelings hurt if they weren't.

I zipped up to the desk, rang the bell and waited. In the middle of the long, empty counter was something that looked like a piece of trash that had been trampled underfoot during the storm. It was thick with mud where it wasn't smudged with black, and it looked so completely out of place, it shocked me. That hotel was *clean.* In the not quite forty eight hours I'd been staying there, I'd never once seen as much as a piece of wastepaper in a hallway or three whole cigarette butts in an ashtray. The maids must have gone through once every five minutes. Whatever it was lying on the counter seemed to me like vandalism.

A door opened at the back and a desk clerk came through, efficient and cheerful. I wondered vaguely where the Inner Harbor got these people. I'd been in hundreds of hotels in my life, and all the others had had at least one sour apple. The Inner Harbor came up with one pleasant clerk after another—and they all knew what they were doing.

This one said, "Good evening, Miss McKenna. I love your sweater." Then she turned around to fish my key out of the slot.

I stared at her back. The sweater was Nick's, but it would have been bad manners to go into all that, and a waste of time. The clerk turned to me with my key in her left hand.

"Nasty day for sightseeing, isn't it?" she said. "It's really too bad you had to come to Baltimore in this weather. It's usually quite pleasant here."

"I remember," I said. "You're the—you checked me in."

"That's right." She practically beamed. "We were so excited when we heard you'd be staying here. We were fighting over that check-in. And we didn't know what you'd be like. But it's been wonderful, really." She faltered. "I don't mean about the, well, the trouble—"

"That's all right," I said.

"I got Miss Damereaux to sign all my books. And Sherry got Tempesta Stewart to. And you've had such an interesting life."

"I could do with a little less interesting sometimes."

"You'll straighten it all out. We have faith in you."

I had a response to that one, but I swallowed it. I have a nasty habit of being sarcastic when what I really want to be is funny, and I knew this woman wasn't someone who would appreciate that sort of thing. People who had *all* Phoebe's books never did. I tucked the key she was handing me into my jeans.

"Did Barbara Defborn talk to you? The police detective? We've been wondering about some messages that showed up—"

She leaned eagerly over the counter. "Are you investigating something? I've never been part of a real murder investigation."

"Barbara Defborn didn't talk to you?"

"If you mean the police, of course they talked to me. And everybody else. But the police don't count, do they?"

For what? I wondered. I said, "I suppose not."

"You'll want to know how it was I wrote your name on that note," she said. "Well, it was strange. It really was." She was delighted that it had been strange. Absolutely delighted. "Normally, when we get a note for a guest, we deliver just as we receive it. That's policy. The privacy of our guests is very important to us. We've delivered all kinds of things. Torn notes. Wet notes. Even smelly notes."

"Smelly notes?"

"With perfume on them."

"Oh," I said.

"But these," she said, "these were impossible. Filthy. And not just filthy. Covered with mud, covered with grime, I couldn't even pick them up. They *oozed.*"

I looked down the counter at the piece of "trash."

"I really couldn't see delivering something like that. I really couldn't. You always have to assume that the way the note gets here is the way the person who sent it wanted it to be—that seems absurd, but it's true. But these. Well, obviously they'd been dropped in the rain and stepped on. I don't think anybody would do that deliberately. And even if they had, I was worried about the reputation of the hotel. Someone might think we'd done it ourselves, and hadn't had the good manners to fix it. So—"

"So you took the note out of the envelope and put it in a hotel envelope."

"I put it in a plain envelope," she corrected. "Not one with a letter-head on it. We keep a few of those around for people who don't want to use printed stationery."

"You threw the envelopes away?"

She flushed. "Yes, I did. If I'd realized—"

"No, no," I said. "I'm not blaming you. I just wanted to be sure. Did you tell Barbara Defborn about all this?"

"The police woman? Yes, I did. If I'd realized—well, I would have told you first. The hotel might not have liked that, but I would have told you first. Of course, we're very conscientious about cooperating with the police, but if I'd known you were interested—"

"You don't understand," I said desperately. "I'm happy you cooperated with the police. I think you ought to cooperate with them again. Right away."

"Pardon me?"

I pointed down the counter. "Over there," I said. "I think we've got another one."

The piece of trash was indeed another note, and it was the worst we'd seen. It was addressed to Christopher Brand. All it said was: YOU DIE YOU DIE YOU DIE YOU DIE. Unlike the notes Tempesta and I received, it did not consist of a few crayon marks on a mostly white sheet of paper. The writing started in the upper left-hand corner and went down the page. YOU DIE YOU DIE YOU DIE YOU DIE YOU DIE. I don't know how many times it was written.

I watched it being folded into a Baggie and packed away in Barbara Defborn's purse. Then I got my cigarettes out and lit up in spite of her disapproval. This was not, after all, a murder scene. The note could have been lying on the counter for all of half an hour. That was how long Donna Grant, the clerk, had been in the back, attending to administrative work while the desk was clear. In the meantime, twenty people had probably come through the lobby, smokers and non-smokers alike. Cigarette butts, footprints, fingerprints, stray pieces of paper: anything the police found now would be useless as evidence. Things could have been brought in and taken out wholesale, and nobody would ever be able to pin down where or when.

I was sitting in the middle of a circular couch, near the ashtray. On the other side of the coffee table sat Nick and Phoebe and Adrienne and Tempesta Stewart, bright-eyed and patient. It's amazing what a first-rate murder mystery can do for the human condition. Adrienne didn't look hungry. Phoebe didn't look sick. Tempesta didn't look bitchy. Even Nick was in a better mood than he should have been. Nick hates seeing me involved in murders. Usually, by this point in an investigation, he's ready to wring my neck. Now, he just looked like he had a headache.

I'd run into them while I'd been pacing around the lobby waiting for Barbara Defborn to arrive. They'd been on their way out to dinner, and I dearly wished to know how Tempesta had managed to get herself invited in on *that*. I'd never had the chance to ask. First I'd had to tell them what I was doing there. Then I'd had to tell them why it was important. Then Barbara walked in.

Barbara put her purse on the table and sat down beside me.

"It's just another note," she said. "I don't think anything's happened yet. You have a right to be tense, but—"

I shook my head. "You don't understand," I said. "I don't think it *is* just another note."

"Then what is it? It can't be a copycat. Unless you think . . ." She lowered her voice and cast a covert glance at Tempesta. "Miss Stewart could be lying," she admitted. "She said she didn't tell anyone but you and Mr. Carras about that note, but she could have told anyone."

"Actually, I don't think so," I said. "I've been having my mind changed about Tempesta lately. I don't think she would lie."

"Religious people lie," Barbara Defborn said. "It happens."

"I'm sure it happens. But when we came on this tour, I just assumed Tempesta was a hypocritical fake. I don't believe that anymore. I'm not worried about the note being copycat. That's not it."

"What is *it?*"

"It's not the same as the other notes. Don't you see?"

"No."

I waved to Nick. He was the only one I wanted, but I'm not stupid. I was going to get all of them and I knew it. They trooped over en masse, Adrienne hanging a little behind as if to stay out of sight and out of danger of being told to go somewhere else. I grabbed her by the arm and pulled her close to me. At the back of my mind, I was forming the half-baked idea that this was therapeutic. If it wasn't, I wanted her as close to me as possible, in case she started to come apart.

"I wish you'd take that thing out of the bag and let us look at it," I told Barbara.

"Procedure," she said firmly. "Sorry."

"I know about procedure." I sighed. "But the thing is— Look. I got a note. What did it say?"

"I know what it said," Adrienne said. " 'You ruin it for everybody. You ought to die.' Or something like that." She took a deep breath. "But it's all right, isn't it? It's not somebody who wants to kill you. It's somebody who wants to kill somebody else and make people think they did it *because* of you."

"How do you know all that?" I asked her.

"Phoebe told me."

Phoebe shrugged. "In the first place," she said, "I don't believe in lying to children. In the second place, I'm going to be sick."

"Again?" Adrienne said.

"Never mind," I said. "The point is, that was one line and all it said was that I 'ought' to be dead. Well, personally I think Ted Bundy ought to be dead, but I'm not going to run out and kill him. We've all got people we think ought to be dead. So what?"

Nick said, "Rapists and murderers and child uh—"

"Child molesters," Adrienne finished for him.

"You ought to think about a good Christian school for that child," Tempesta said.

"Forget the good Christian school. She'd be expelled in a week. Think about *your* note."

"Mine?" Tempesta frowned. "I don't even remember. It was nonsense."

"It was nonsense, but it was the same as mine," I said. "You 'ought' to be dead. And that's what worries me about Christopher Brand's. There's no 'ought' about it. It says 'you die.' It's not even a threat. It's a statement of fact."

"I wouldn't go to a good Christian school anyway," Adrienne said. "They wouldn't take Courtney."

"Who's Courtney?" Tempesta said.

"Courtney Feinberg. She's Adrienne's best friend. Can't any of you people stick to the subject?"

Barbara Defborn could. She had opened her purse and taken out the Baggie with the filth-encrusted envelope in it. She had laid the Baggie on the coffee table. Now she was staring at it, undecided.

" 'You die,' " she said.

"Whoever set this up meant to make it look like a series of nut killings," I said. "Meant to make it seem as if the people he or she killed weren't the targets in any real sense. Meant to make it look random. Homicidal rage, striking out without direction."

"I *know* that," Barbara Defborn said.

"But this isn't meant to look like that at all," I went on. "Either that, or by the time whoever it is got to Christopher Brand, it was just too much. There's rage in that note, Barbara, real rage, not the political kind. Whoever that is hates Christopher Brand. And Christopher Brand is out on the streets somewhere, getting totally blotto in tenth-rate bars. You remember what you said about Mrs. Keeley being drugged?"

"Of course I remember," Barbara said. "We got the report back on Miss Kleig, too. She was full of methaqualone. But that doesn't help us, Patience. The Darvocet Mrs. Keeley took came right out of a pill bottle in her own purse. And the methaqualone—"

"Don't tell me Evelyn was kiting on Quaaludes," I said. "I won't believe it."

"She wasn't. But methaqualone is a common prescription for some kinds of depression. It's supposed to be controlled, but you know what that is. Doctors hand the stuff out right and left. At least two members of the tour have it—Hazel Ganz and Ivy Samuels Tree. Miss Tree has been spending all her time with the Association of Afro-American Writers. Miss Ganz has been out more than she's been in. We're checking it, but it's going to come down to somebody lifting a bottle out of somebody else's purse. Just you watch."

"With Christopher Brand, it's not going to have to come to even that," I said. "Nobody's going to need to drug him. The man's a full-fledged alcoholic and he's dead set on having the world's most amazing binge. In another hour, he's going to be comatose all on his own."

"And vulnerable," Barbara Defborn said.

"If he gets anywhere near this group, he will be," I agreed. "I was cursing him out half an hour ago, but I'm beginning to be grateful. At least this gives us some time. He was at a place called the Green Door the last time I saw him. He might still be there. If he isn't, we'll know the kind of place to look."

"What do you mean, look?" Amelia Samson's voice boomed across the lobby, a cannon that had somehow acquired a fake British accent. "You don't have to look. I know exactly where he is."

# TWENTY

The trouble with Amelia, in my opinion, is that she's always been an irresistible force. Physically, mentally, vocally, emotionally—if there's an immovable object in the universe that might counter her effect, it hasn't been found. She came sweeping up to us in all that metal-wire underconstruction and all those beads, the vision of a nineteenth-century matriarch with a nasty mind. Maybe that's what she always wanted to be. The second half of the twentieth century has never sat too well with Amelia. It lacks the rewards of periods with more rigid hierarchies.

She gave Nick one of her Looks, causing him to say "shit" under his breath and scoot sideways on the couch. She gave Tempesta another one, but didn't get the same effect. Tempesta had to deal with Amelia almost daily on AWR business, and she was used to the act. The far semicircular couch being empty, Amelia marched over to that. Then she sat down in it as if it had been made for her and pounded on the carpet with her cane. The cane was a new wrinkle. It had surfaced on and off during the tour. It had a silver knob and a mahogany shaft and a lot of carving near the base. I had never seen her use it to walk with. She just carried it around with her and waved it for emphasis. Or pounded it, as she was doing now.

Actually, I would have been a little uncomfortable if Amelia had used that cane to walk with. Amelia had been a part of my life so long, I couldn't help thinking of her as eternal. And as eternally strong. Amelia had been a draft animal all her life—in her father's house before she married; at the steam laundry in the days when she'd been poor; at the typewriter ever since. There had been a time when I hadn't thought any of that to be true. After all, these days Amelia wrote only plot outlines—she had two dozen secretaries who turned the outlines into books—and she wrote those in bed at that. I'd come to understand that the impression of ease and luxury and self-indulgence was illusory. Amelia's fans expected her to live like a queen. She did her best to oblige them.

She pounded her cane on the floor again and looked straight at Phoebe. "Have you got your hands on that young man yet? If you have, I think you should turn him over to me."

"We're straightening it out," Phoebe said hastily.

"No, we're not," Nick said. "All we've done is found him."

"Hiding under a rock somewhere, of course," Amelia said.

"Hiding out in his cabin in Vermont," Nick said. "Having a moral crisis. Or so he says."

"Bull manure," Amelia said.

"My feelings exactly," Nick said.

"You know what you ought to do with him?" Amelia's eyes shone. "You ought to call his mother and tell her the whole story. Beginning to end. That's what you ought to do. Isn't she the one who gave me the lecture about how civilization was crumbling because men no longer understood it was their duty to do right by the girls they got in trouble? The one at the party Phoebe gave last New Year's?"

"Yeah," Nick said. "And she loves Phoebe. *And* she's desperate for grandchildren. *And* she's got a niece with Down's syndrome she absolutely dotes on."

"Better and better," Amelia said.

"Oh God," Phoebe said.

"Never let them get you thinking they're invulnerable," Amelia said. "They're not. And never let them get away with bullshit. The New Morality. Horse feathers. Biggest con game in the history of sex. Take the bastard apart. He's asking for it."

"Is there something going on around here I don't know about?" Barbara Defborn said.

I got out another cigarette and lit up again. It was starting. Whenever I got anywhere near these people, I got dizzy.

"Could we get to Christopher Brand?" I said. "If he's not at the bar, where is he?"

"He's on his way to The Butler Did It," Amelia said. "I ran into him down on Charles Street outside the First Federal Bank. They have one of those machines you can put your Visa card in. Drunk as a skunk and high as a kite, as we used to say when I was growing up. I suppose that's banal. Anyway, he said he was going down to The Butler Did It to sign some books for Gail. She called me, too, although she didn't seem to be in the kind of hurry to get *me* she was in to get Christopher Brand. All she said to *me* was that she wanted to reschedule the signing before we left, not that she wanted me to come in tonight."

"That's right," Phoebe said. "She does want to reschedule the signing. I talked to her this evening. But I'm sure she said she wanted to reschedule the *whole* signing. To have all of us there together. And not tonight."

"Well, he was potted," Amelia said. "And his usual objectionable self. He got it mixed up. Maybe we should call Gail and warn her."

"At the store?" Phoebe was still confused.

"Of course at the store," Amelia said. "I think pregnancy has addled your brain."

"No, it hasn't," Phoebe said. "She's not going to be at the store. She told me. She thought she'd have the place cleaned up and ready to open tonight, but she couldn't get it done. God, she sounded like she was losing her mind. She said she'd do a bunch of stuff, run around like crazy, and then come back and find it wasn't done at all. I don't know. It was confusing and she wasn't making a lot of sense. But she did say she was going to lock up and go out to dinner and just relax for a while. With her—POSSSL-Q?"

"Dan," I said absently. I caught Nick's eye and saw that he was thinking just what I was. Neither one of us liked this at all.

Amelia was going on. "It's like I said. He was potted. Reeling around and hardly able to stand up. I don't know how he's going to get all the way out to North Charles. He'll probably have to walk. There isn't a cabdriver in the world who would pick him up. This tour has been an absolute mess. Everybody on it is crazy."

"Everybody means everybody," Tempesta said.

Amelia ignored her. "I leave the hotel to go to the bank, who do I meet? Mr. Lowry, all frantic because he has to go make funeral arrangements, or shipping arrangements, and he wants to buy flowers for the bag she's going to be shipped in—I'm not making this up—and he can't, because he doesn't have time to stop and buy them and he can't get them over the phone like a normal person because he doesn't have a credit card. Do you believe Mr. Jonathon Hancock Lowry doesn't have a credit card?"

"Yes," I said.

"Well, apparently it's true," Amelia said, "although it took a little while to convince *me* of it. So he hands me a fifty-dollar bill and asks me to pick something up. Pick something up, for God's sake. I took the fifty dollars and I called a florist. They gave me some song and dance about how they couldn't deliver until tomorrow morning, but I took care of *that.*"

"I'll bet you did," I said. I felt sorry for the florist.

Amelia was going on. "So I call the florist from the lobby phone," she said, "and when I come out of there I run into Hazel. I'm beginning to think nervous breakdowns are a communicable disease. Anyway, she's over near the elevators, and when she sees me she starts waving and shouting and jumping up and down, and when I get there all she wants to talk about is her taxes. Her taxes this, her taxes that. I—"

"Taxes?" Nick said.

"I don't understand why so many people have trouble with their taxes," Amelia said. "I've been doing my own for years and I've never had any trouble. I got audited once and they owed me money. Of course they did. I always build that in. I don't understand why everybody doesn't."

"Not everybody makes enough money to afford to pay more taxes than they have to," Phoebe said. "For God's sake, Amelia."

"Taxes," I said slowly. There are times when thinking seems to me to be a physical act. I could feel the machinery grinding, the muscle flexing—isn't the brain supposed to be a muscle? Or something like it. Suddenly, I felt very stupid.

"Amelia," I said, "what was it *exactly* about Hazel's taxes? *Exactly.*"

"How am I supposed to know what it was *exactly?*" Amelia snorted. "You know Hazel. She gets on a subject and she just can't get off. Author's lending rights. Pseudonyms in romance publishing. Exclusivity clauses. She goes on and on and on."

"Yes, but what did she *say?*"

"What she *said* was, she came back from being out, and she had a note in her box to call her lawyer back in Cleveland. So she called him, and he told her he'd had a letter from the IRS. And that was as far as I got with the common sense, because after that she was talking gibberish. Sheer gibberish. Did you ever hear of something called the Children's Crusade for Animal Rights?"

I blanched. "Oh yes," I said.

"Well, I don't believe it. There's nothing of the sort. Especially since — Do you know what Hazel said? She said it was all about giving pets the vote."

"It was about doing away with dog pounds," I sighed. "At least, that was what it was when I heard about it." I turned to Nick. "Did your friend from the IRS ever call back? Do you know what my letter was about?"

"Yeah," Nick said, "as a matter of fact, I do. They're going to disallow a deduction to something called the Victims' Rights League. But it's all right. They're not going to audit. They just want—"

"How can they know what to disallow if they don't audit?" Amelia demanded.

"We always list my charitable deductions," I said. "A lot of people do that. There's been so much tax fraud with those it sometimes saves a lot of time and trouble if you spell it out and back it up when you have a big number for that line. And I always have a big number. Between my mother and Evelyn, I've been giving away a third of everything I earn."

"Guilt," Amelia said wisely. "All you young women nowadays. Guilt. We didn't have women's lib when I was growing up, but we at least had sense. We made our livings because we had to. We didn't get all hot and bothered when we were good at it. Now there's this women's lib and you all run around driving yourselves crazy when you think you're making too much money."

Barbara Defborn stirred beside me on the couch. "Wait a minute," she said. "Are you saying there's been fraud? This charity you're all collecting for is a fraud?"

"Exactly," I said.

"But that's wonderful." She heard herself and got flustered. "I don't mean it's wonderful," she said. "Of course, it's awful for anyone to be taken in like that. But—a motive. We've finally got a motive. Miss Kleig found out about the fraud and whoever was doing the defrauding killed her. And Mrs. Keeley—"

"Stop," I said. "I did that, too. You can't get anywhere that way. It's backwards."

"Backwards?" Barbara Defborn said.

"Why would Evelyn discover the fraud?" Amelia said. "Wasn't the

Victims' Rights League one of hers? Why would she discover this one when she hadn't discovered that one?"

"She didn't discover anything," I said. "She was the fraud."

"What?" Three whats—Nick's and Amelia's and Barbara Defborn's.

"She was the fraud," I repeated. "She engineered the whole thing. Every time. With the Ad Hoc Committee for Advocacy for the Homeless. With the Victims' Rights League. With the Children's Crusade for Animal Rights. All of it. None of them were real. It was right in front of my face all the time and I never even saw it."

"I still don't see it," Nick said. "This is the first time we've had any trouble."

"What tax year?"

"Nineteen eighty-six."

"Exactly. Nineteen eighty-six was the year after Evelyn became my publicist at AST. And I was like everyone else. She never seemed to pay much attention to being a publicist. She was always involved in one charity or another. Her strongest commitment was to the outside work. But she was my publicist. She took a paycheck every week. It never even occurred to me that charity was anything more for her than a particularly compelling hobby. Why should it? People tend to believe what they're told, and what they think they see. It's like what happens when identical twins get together and try to confuse people about which is which. If you think you know you're looking at Person A, you discount contradictory evidence unless it hits you right in the face or gets too overwhelming to be ignored. Evelyn was a lousy publicist—except for her charities. Evelyn was lazy as hell—except when she was working for her charities. Evelyn didn't have the sense of a gnat—except when it came to her charities. I had a million explanations for it. The one I never thought of was that she didn't care about her job because she didn't have to. She didn't intend to have it for long. All she was doing was making sure it looked like she had a legitimate source of income while she was raking in the real money. If she hadn't gotten greedy, she'd have been gone without a trace before any of us heard from the federal government. You know how long these things take. Six months ago, she could have dropped out of sight without a word, and nobody would have bothered to look for her. And when it did come out and they did start looking, she would have been gone."

"But you can't know any of this," Barbara Defborn protested. "You just can't. You're making leaps all over the place."

"I know I am," I said. "But I'm right. Check it out. It's the only way this will make sense."

"It destroys any sense any of it might have made," Barbara said. "Why would somebody kill her? Turn her in, I can see that. Even kidnap her and hold her until the cops could pick her up—if somebody was mad enough about being cheated, I could see that. It's a bit off the wall, but people get that way. But why—"

"He didn't want to turn her in," I said. "If he turned her in, everybody would find out, and that's just what he didn't want."

"But everybody was going to find out anyway," Barbara insisted. "There was so much fraud. What do you think this guy was going to do, wipe out half the Treasury Department and all the bunco squads in five states?"

"He didn't know there was this much fraud," I said. "He hadn't known her very long. He probably thought this was it. After she was dead, he could take care of it. He could take over the organization. He could fix things. At least he had a chance. As long as she was alive, he didn't have any."

*"Who?"* Tempesta Stewart said. "Who are you talking about?"

I turned to Amelia. "Do you have that fifty-dollar bill Jon Lowry gave you?"

"Of course I do. Only supermarkets and liquor stores take fifty-dollar bills. And Saks, of course, but Saks isn't open at this time of night. What did you think I'd done with it? Torn it up?"

"Show it to me."

Amelia looked as if she wanted to have me committed, but she reached for her purse. It was a mammoth thing covered with beads and embroidery, and she had to search through it for a while. Finally, she came up with an oversized checkbook wallet with her name tooled into the leather and a gold-plated heart for a clasp.

"You want me to reach in here, find the fifty-dollar bill Jon Lowry gave me and hand it to you."

"That's right," I said.

"You're nuts," she said. "I always knew it."

She popped the heart clasp, dug into the bill compartment and came up with a fifty.

"Have it," she said.

I took it. I rubbed my fingertips across the surface. I spit on them. Then I held them out for everyone to see.

In the glossy places where my spit had settled, my fingertips were slowly turning blue.

# TWENTY-ONE

Phoebe wanted to come along, but I wouldn't let her. Adrienne wanted to come along, but I wouldn't let her either, and because she was there I managed to convince Phoebe to stay at the hotel. Barbara Defborn ran off to call her support troops. Nick and I ran out to catch a cab. We left Tempesta and Amelia to fend for themselves. I wasn't going to waste time arguing them out of coming if they wanted to be stupid enough to follow us. I just kept thinking about crazy old Gertrude Lowry and that fortress of a house with its barbed wire and security guards. Schizophrenia, schizophrenia, schizophrenia. Schizophrenia ran in families.

I sat in the cab, wishing like hell Barbara Defborn had been willing to take us with her. Like every other cop I'd ever run across, she was happy enough to have my help until the moment came for the kill. Then she wanted me to disappear. She had a lot more sense, and a lot more class, than Tony Marsh or Lu Martinez. She didn't argue. She didn't lecture. She just disappeared herself. I had the feeling Nick would have disappeared at the same time if I hadn't been holding on to his arm. He certainly didn't want to be in that cab with me.

"This is crazy," he kept saying. "There are people who are paid to do this."

I ignored him, at least on that point. The cab was poking along, making me nuts. The streets were full of people coming out to see what decent weather looked like. The Christmas decorations seemed to be multiplying themselves. There were tinsel and lights and little glass bulbs everywhere, and on the steps of at least two churches there were choirs. Christmas is my favorite season. The week between it and New Year's is the time I wait for every year. I just couldn't get into the spirit. I thought I was going to erupt.

I leaned into the front seat, asked the driver if I could smoke and got permission. I leaned back again and started digging around for cigarettes.

"I can see the headlines in New York already," I said, "and it's all so stupid, because I'm an ass."

"You're an ass to be doing this," Nick agreed. "Where do you think we're going? What do you think we're going to do when we get there?"

Since he knew perfectly well where we were going—he'd heard me tell the driver to take us out to The Butler Did It—I let this pass, too. "It was there all the time," I said. "You gave it to me this morning. Jon Lowry gave it to me. And the business about the fraud—Christopher Brand did everything but hit me over the head with it and I never knew a thing."

"Right," Nick said.

"That chalk," I said. "That chalk was on the money Jon Lowry had in the manila envelope he gave to Phoebe. Phoebe didn't open the envelope, but I did. I got the stuff on my hands. You were right. It doesn't really stick too well. But it got into the creases between my fingers and my palms, and it lasted there long enough to get wet. Then it stuck just fine. It was damn near impossible to get off."

"Why would there be architect's chalk on Jon Lowry's money?" Nick demanded. "I told you they *used* to use it in kidnapping cases in the thirties. I also told you they gave that up."

"Because Jon Lowry really is crazy, as crazy as his aunt ever was. And because he told me."

"Excuse me?" Nick said.

"He didn't tell me in so many words." My lighter caught, died, caught. I dragged hard to get my cigarette going and didn't quite make it. I gave up for the moment. "He kept ranting and raving at me outside the garage about how nobody ever took him seriously and all the things his lawyers did to him and God knows what else. That was the key to the whole thing. He must have been driving his financial people crazy for years. Did he tell you what he did with his money?"

"About putting it in cash and gold?" Nick said. "He didn't tell me, but I heard about it. From my friend at the IRS, if you want to know the truth. I almost admire him for it. Tax law is the biggest pile of slime—"

"You've told me, you've told me. But I don't blame the banks. They've got to protect themselves and Jon Lowry is not stable. Anybody who talks to him for any length of time begins to see that. He's paranoid as all hell, and he resents like crazy being treated like a child. Or an incompetent. That's what Aunt Gertrude did to him, all his life. He didn't want to file tax forms because he didn't want to give out information about himself—"

"I don't want to give out information about myself either," Nick said, "and if the courts hadn't decided that the IRS was immune to the Constitution, I wouldn't have to."

"Don't lecture," I said. "There was a good reason why he didn't want to give out information about himself. He was just as feeble at all this stuff as his financial people said he was. Worse, probably. I'll bet there's been legal action, too. Attempts to get control of the money away from him. Attempts to get him committed."

"Good guess," Nick said. "Not about the commitment but about the other thing. The Toliver-Campion Trust filed suit twice. The first time, they wanted control of the money. The second time, they just wanted him the hell out of their bank. But they lost both, Pay."

"I assumed they had," I said. "I also assume a little extra evidence— like Jon falling for a con artist for big money—wouldn't hurt their chances if they wanted to go to court a third time. But I doubt if any of that matters. Because what Jon cares about is what they think of him. It's absolutely crucial to him that he's not perceived as a fool. Which is why he was so angry about the chalk. He knew about it. He knew the bank had done it to him. He knew why. We were standing outside that garage and Evelyn's body was inside in a bag, for God's sake, and all he could talk about was all the terrible things people had done to him. How they'd treated him. What an idiot they thought he was. He was distraught all right, but it wasn't out of grief. He was angry as hell."

"About Evelyn or the chalk?"

"About both. Evelyn for cheating him. The chalk because he knew the bank had put it there just in case he was idiot enough to give the key to one of his safety-deposit boxes to somebody else or fall for a gold-mine scheme or something. I'll bet if you check the bank in Baltimore where he's got his box you'll find some old guy at the head of the safety-deposit room. Or some older woman. Someone who would have known about this particular method of tracing money. Whatever. Other banks had probably tried other things."

"Does he have a bank in Baltimore?"

"Does it matter? Maybe he picked the envelope up in New York. He gave it to Phoebe to hold. I just assumed he must have picked it up here. He has to have those boxes all over the place. He doesn't have credit cards and he doesn't have accounts he can wire off to in an emergency. Whatever. That's not the point, Nick."

"The point is that you're making this up."

"It fits. It works. It will check out. You just watch. At any rate, Evelyn never intended to be around long enough to get caught for the frauds. She started in 1985. I'd guess she intended to be out of sight by the beginning of 1988. Instead, into her life came Mr. Jonathon Hancock Lowry and eight hundred fifty million dollars. He was shy. He was awkward. He would have followed any woman anywhere if he could have been made to believe she fell for him before she knew about his money. Either Evelyn didn't know about his money in the beginning or she was a damn good actress. In fact, we both know she was a damn good actress. Whatever the sequence, he got caught. She had a chance to milk him good and she wasn't going to let it go."

"Why not just marry him?" Nick said. "Everyone said he was crazy about her."

"What was going to happen when all that fraud started coming out? Besides, I don't think she really liked him much. And she was greedy, but she wasn't entirely stupid. She didn't need the whole eight hundred fifty million. She just needed enough of it. She could get that without having to put up with him in bed."

Nick thought about it. "All right," he said. "That I'll buy."

"Good. Buy this, too. The first kick came in Minneapolis. Christopher Brand got a call from *his* lawyer when we were in Minneapolis. It had to have been about this. I assumed it was the Ad Hoc Committee he'd heard about, because he was checking that out, but it must have been one of the others. And there are a few things you ought to know about Christopher. In the first place, he couldn't stand Evelyn. He thought she was running him like a slave. In the second place, he absolutely hates Jon Lowry. Hates him. All that inherited money and unearned status blows Christopher's corks completely. Up until Minneapolis, he was nice to both of them. He had to be. After Minneapolis, he was in the clear. He had Evelyn just where he wanted her. Not that he was satisfied with that."

"Christopher Brand isn't satisfied with anything," Nick said. "He—well, never mind what he did. It was in the breakfast room this morning. It concerned hash brown potatoes. It was incredible."

"Christopher usually is," I said. "And since what he really wanted was revenge, damn the practical consequences, I think he did what he thought was a very smart thing."

"What?"

"Went right out and told Jon Lowry just what Evelyn was and what she was doing."

"*McKenna.* That would make him not just crazy, but stupid. He could have blackmailed the hell out of Evelyn just by threatening to tell Lowry what he knew."

"I know. But you're making an assumption. You've decided that getting at Evelyn would be Christopher's main purpose. She controlled the tour. She could help or hurt his career. How much do you think Christopher Brand cares about his career? He mouths off about it a lot, but every time he's ever had a choice between it and anything else, he's chosen the anything else. He didn't care about Evelyn. He cares about what all drunks care about, and never forget that Christopher Brand is a drunk. He cares about cosmic truth and cosmic justice and getting the universe to fork over what he thinks it owes him. Making Jon Lowry feel small was much more important to him than blackmailing Evelyn would ever be. Besides, he'd have it around longer. Evelyn was going to make tracks eventually. He'd dealt with enough greedy women to realize that."

"So Christopher told Jon and Jon confronted Evelyn?"

"Exactly."

"Why didn't he just walk out?"

"He didn't want to walk out. He wanted to erase the whole business. He wanted to make sure nobody would ever know he'd been fooled. I don't know what he told her to keep her from bolting, but he must have told her something. Maybe just that he didn't believe it. He had all that lovely money to use for bait."

"If he was going to kill her anyway, why wait for Baltimore? Wasn't Minneapolis early in the tour?"

"Baltimore was the only city we were scheduled in that wasn't a hectic mess. All the rest of them were one interview after the other, one party after the other. This was the only place we had any time.

He's been dropping messages off at the reception desk, stealing prescription drugs out of people's handbags, chasing all over the place—I'll bet my life he followed Christopher to that God-awful place we were at this afternoon, and to the bar later, too. The neighborhood looked deserted, but you know how that is. You can never tell. And it was better not to wait until we got back to New York. She might have skipped out by then. Anything could have happened."

"He killed Evelyn because she knew," Nick said slowly. "Just because she knew. Is that what you're saying?"

"Exactly."

"And he's on his way to kill Christopher Brand because *he* knows."

"Right again."

"Then why in the name of God did he kill Margaret Keeley?"

I blew a stream of smoke into the air. "He killed her because she knew, too," I said. "And don't tell me that's farfetched, because it's nothing of the kind. We've been hearing about Margaret ever since we got here. Gail Larson told me she was a snoop. Gail Larson also told me Margaret was very good at finding out scandal, as long as it wasn't sex scandal. When it came to sex, she let her prejudices get in the way of her instincts. In every other situation, her instincts were excellent. And she did snoop. Into everything. As a matter of course. Christopher Brand found the People's Center for Social Action and got the whole history of their problems with the Ad Hoc Committee for Advocacy for the Homeless. I think Margaret Keeley did, too. There's a little girl over there, Darcy Penter. All we have to do is ask her."

"Even if I give you that, how did Jon *know* she knew?"

"The same way everybody knew what she knew," I said. "She told him. Phoebe saw her on the street that afternoon she was murdered. She was probably waiting for Evelyn. They were supposed to meet *somewhere* and go to The Butler Did It together, and Phoebe said Mrs. Keeley was checking her watch and peering around as if she was expecting someone. I'd guess Jon had killed Evelyn by that time and stuck her body in Tempesta's rent-a-car trunk. We can get Barbara Defborn to work through all that business about where it was parked and where Jon and Evelyn were and all the rest of it. I'm pretty sure that when he went to meet Margaret Keeley, he was alone. He told her Evelyn had sent him to pick her up and take her over to The Butler Did It, and they went. Evelyn didn't have any keys on her when she was found. Then when they got to the store, he let her set up and fed her drugged coffee or something while she was doing it, and when she finally passed out he killed her."

"You got all this from knowing who was committing fraud and where a lot of architect's chalk came from?"

"I got it from being able to make sense in a systematic manner," I said, "which I can do even if you and Lu Martinez think I can't. Gracie Allen, my foot. Things like this are rigid, really. Once you have the one or two really important facts, you start at the beginning and there's only one way to go. Aren't we there?"

The cab had started to slow. Nick leaned forward to peer out the windshield. I leaned sideways to look out the window. Up front, the cabdriver said, "Police bar—oh *hell.*"

"What?" I said.

"Put that *out,*" Nick said.

He grabbed my cigarette and started to crush it in the ashtray on his side, over and over again, as if he were trying to beat it to death. I grabbed his arm.

"What are you doing?" I shouted at him. "What do you think you—"

"Smell," he commanded.

"Smell what?"

The cigarette was out. He leaned over my lap, grabbed the window handle and rolled. Cold air came pouring onto my face, tinged with the liquid afterglow of rain. Something else came pouring in, too—a smell, yes, but the kind of smell that feels as thick and tactile as mayonnaise and always makes you choke.

The street was full of gas.

# TWENTY-TWO

They had cordoned off the whole block, from the beauty parlor to Sun's Wigs and Gifts and the Jewish Council Thrift Shop. They had put up sawhorses and body lines of uniformed patrolmen. They had evacuated everyone they could find. It was nearly seven and after closing time for many of the businesses, but prime take-in hours for others. People were standing at the edges of the sectioned-off area, looking frightened and confused. Nobody looked interested in leaving, although the uniforms kept trying to convince them to. The rainbow-surfaced ribbon of gasoline was stagnant and beautiful, standing motionless like a fairy pond in the middle of the street. There had to be ten or fifteen gallons of it, maybe more. It shimmered in the light from the streetlamps, like a liquid Christmas decoration.

Nick wanted me to stay in the cab. I hadn't listened to him up until then, and I wasn't going to listen to him now. I got out and walked along the perimeter until I saw Barbara Defborn, crisp and business-like in her little black suit, standing next to one of the patrol cars. She had a hand mike in her hand and was talking into it, probably to somebody at headquarters. I headed in her direction and saw something I hadn't noticed before: the fire engines. There were stupefying numbers of fire engines. Every fire engine in Baltimore must have been standing by just beyond that block, and maybe every fire engine in the county. I couldn't help wondering what would happen if somebody's house caught fire.

I wedged my way through a couple of knots of spectators, ducked under the flailing arms of a patrolman trying to explain something with his hands and came to a stop next to Barbara Defborn. She saw me standing there and nearly spit.

"You didn't *tell* me he was crazy," she said. "This guy is a world-class Looney Tune."

"There didn't seem to be time to talk back at the hotel."

"Shit."

I edged a little away from her, just in case she decided to resort to physical violence. She seemed capable of it. "Have you figured out what happened yet? Do you know how the gas got into the street?"

"Oh, we know how the gas got into the street," Barbara said. "He may be Looney Tunes, but he's a smart son of a bitch. He went over there"—she pointed to the gas station in the middle of the block—"and walked into the office and told them he was going to hand-pump twenty dollars' worth. Then he came back out here, took the nozzle off the pump, rigged it open with a little tape and put it down on the ground just to this side of the tank. I *don't* know where he got the car. He might have stolen it. We didn't want to hang around in there and check it out."

"I don't blame you," I said. "Is it going to blow?"

"If your friend has anything to say about it, it is. He's sitting in that building over there"—she pointed to The Butler Did It—"threatening to light a match. Which is why the fire boys aren't in there cleaning this mess up."

"What about Christopher Brand?"

"Your guess is as good as mine. We haven't seen him."

I swallowed hard. "I think I'd get out of here if I were you," I said. "He's got no reason not to blow it. Not a single one."

"What about staying alive?"

"Not in this case. The whole thing happened in the first place because he has a pathological need not to get caught doing things he doesn't want people to know he's doing. Sort of."

"Oh, *fine.*"

She dropped the hand mike and walked away. Moments later, she was talking to one of the firemen, gesticulating wildly and marking her points by stamping her foot.

I moved away from the patrol car, toward the barrier rather than away from it. I might not have gotten very far, but the patrolman at that point in the line was one of the ones I'd already met and he let me approach. Behind me, I could hear Nick's deep-throated bass booming into the silence.

"McKenna! Get away from there! What do you think you're doing?"

I got as close as I could. I wanted a good look at The Butler Did It's front windows. Barbara had said Jon Lowry was in there, but I could see no sign of him. The store was dark. The streetlamps reflected into the plate glass. I squinted and turned my head and tried a half dozen different angles, but either there was nothing to see or I just couldn't see it. My arms and legs and back and neck were going through agonies of spasms. I tried shaking them out, and then did what I always did when I got too scared to do anything else. I took a deep breath.

It was one of the biggest mistakes of my life. I've seen half a dozen B movies with gas spills in them, but never one that let on what the fumes were like. They didn't just smell awful, they hurt. They ripped right into my lungs as if I'd tried to breathe sandpaper. I gagged and choked and shut down respiration as far as I could. My body wanted air. It kept trying to get it. It got more sandpaper instead.

I backed up automatically. I couldn't help myself. I stumbled over a wandering cop and accidentally kicked the shins of a stray fireman. The fireman had a gas mask on, and an oxygen tank. I didn't blame him.

I hit one of the patrol cars and came to a stop, my eyes tearing. I'd never felt so awful in my life. I would have thrown up if I could have, but I hadn't eaten anything all day. There was nothing in there to heave. I sat down on the patrol car's bumper and put my head between my legs, just to see if it would work. It didn't.

When I came upright again, Nick was standing beside me. He looked exasperated.

"Don't put your head down there," he snapped. "The fumes are heavier down there. You're going to make it worse."

"Thanks for telling me," I said. "Christ, Nick, how can he still be alive in there? Why hasn't he suffocated yet?"

"Just look at him."

I followed Nick's pointing finger. This time, I found Jonathon Hancock Lowry with no trouble at all. He was hanging off The Butler Did It's six-foot-tall sign, wedged up there between the ground floor and the second by what looked like sheer force of will. I supposed he had to be holding on to, or sitting on, something. I just couldn't see what.

"He's just far enough up so the wind's pulling most of it away from him," Nick said. "He could stay up there damn near forever."

"But what's he doing?"

"How the hell am I supposed to know?"

"Do you know anything?" I asked him.

"I came with you, McKenna. I know if he starts screaming 'top of the world, Ma,' I'm going to duck."

"There's Gail Larson," I said. "She looks bad."

He stepped aside to let her come between us, and she smiled at him in a distracted way that said her manners were glued on but nothing else was. I'd always thought of her as a pretty woman, but she'd lost it in the crisis. Her blond hair was thick with sweat and hanging down the back of her neck. The skin on her face was red in patches and dead white in others. She was shaking crazily under a thick coat that looked like it could have kept out the cold in an Alaskan blizzard.

"My God," she said, "I don't even know if I'm insured for this."

"You can sue his estate," Nick said drily. "I'll even represent you. Christ knows, the money will be there to collect."

"What's that?" Gail said.

We all turned to look, but we needn't have. Christopher Brand had a voice as deep and loud as Nick's, and stronger. It exploded over the block like something coming through a bullhorn. Christopher Brand had no bullhorn. He just had himself, and the crazy recklessness that had been the shape and tenor of his life.

"What's *wrong* with you people?" he shouted. "What are you standing around for? He's going to blow the place up!"

I jerked my head around to look at the sign and caught Jon Lowry just as he moved. He didn't move so much as convulse. His body bent double and jackknifed straight again. For a few long seconds, he looked as if he were standing on thin air.

Jon Lowry did not have a deep voice. He did have panic, and craziness, and fear.

"You're dead," he screamed. "You're dead you're *dead* you're DEAD."

"You're NUTS," Christopher screamed back.

Jon clutched at his clothes, fumbling and clawing at himself. Somebody switched on a searchlight and pointed it straight at him. Suddenly, I could see him plain, the metal bar he was standing on, the way his body was wedged against the brick. He couldn't see anything at all. The light poured into his eyes and he blinked, squinted, shuddered. He clutched at his face and shook his head, as if that would help. Most important of all, he started to slip.

Christopher Brand saw it first, and for once in my life I didn't condemn him for the reflexive thoughtlessness that had been the contrapuntal theme of his life. I would have blown it—thought the whole thing through, wasted time, thrown away my chance. Christopher Brand just moved. He was surprisingly fast for a drunk with a pipe and cigarette habit, surprisingly fast for anyone. He went running up under the sign and jumped.

I didn't think he was going to make it. For some reason, I assumed he'd have to get high enough to get a firm grip and tackle Jon from there. The sign was well off the street. I was as tall as Christopher and Nick was taller, and I didn't believe either of us would have made it.

Christopher Brand was smarter than I was, that time as well. He wasn't trying to get a hold. He was just trying to make himself a nuisance. The first time up he slapped his hand against the sole of Jon Lowry's shoe. The second time he caught a lace and tried to pull. Jon kicked air, ruining his balance even more than he had when he'd jerked out of control under the assault of light.

"Get DOWN off of there," Christopher was yelling. "Get DOWN. What the HELL do you think you're DOING, you little SHIT?"

"Oh God," I heard Barbara Defborn say, her voice coming out of the darkness as if from another room. "He's going to blow it. We're all going to end up on the moon."

"CRAP," Christopher Brand said.

He took one more leap into the air. He put both his hands out this time, and managed to get Jon on the shin of his right leg. In the searchlight's glare I could see the pack of matches, held aloft as if they were what Christopher was reaching for. The hand that was clutching them flailed, hit the brick of the building and swung forward. The arm the hand was attached to wrapped itself around the edge of the sign and went rigid. Christopher Brand jumped one more time and Jon jerked, even though he hadn't been touched. His match hand cramped and uncramped, cramped and uncramped, and I saw it. It looked like a plain square pack of matches of the size sold by the hundred in boxes in novelty stores, and it went floating to the street like an oversized flake of snow.

Christopher Brand walked over to it and picked it up. "Jesus Christ," he said. "What's wrong with you people? This guy has to be some kind of lunatic."

It would have been the anticlimax of all time, except that that was when the sirens started up.

Maybe they should have turned them on at the beginning. As soon as he heard them, Jonathon Hancock Lowry fainted dead away.

# EPILOGUE

Just about a week later, on the day Adrienne and I were getting ready to leave for the country, David Grossman came to my door looking for Phoebe. When the bell rang, I thought it was my mother's driver—again. Phoebe had recovered sufficiently from morning sickness and depression by the time we got back to New York to help Adrienne pack. Because of that, Garrison had already made six trips between car and apartment and was likely to make six more. I was standing in the kitchen with the door to the hallway shut tight, looking down at the stack of New York *Post*s my mother had sent up with the car and trying to tell Phoebe and Nick what Barbara Defborn's phone call had been about. Barbara Defborn had woken me up at six forty-five that morning. It was an event strangely in keeping with all the rest of it: to have anything to do with Evelyn Nesbitt Kleig, at any time or for any reason, was to be denied the comfort of sleep.

The *Post*s were the ones I hadn't seen, the ones that came out when we were still in Baltimore. The headlines said: KILLER FIEND LOOSE. The explanatory banners said: NEW YORK'S LOVE GIRL DETECTIVE TO HELP BALTIMORE POLICE SOLVE MOST DIABOLICAL CRIME IN CITY'S HISTORY. I kept trying to figure out how they'd managed to get that immense sentence into such large type and still fit it onto the page. Of course, there was nothing *else* on the page but the short headline and a large picture of me, but the *Post* thought I was a celebrity.

I pushed the papers away across the kitchen table. "I think I liked this thing better when Rupert Murdoch owned it," I said. "At least Murdoch's people got the facts straight."

"How can you say Murdoch's people got the facts straight?" Nick said. "Last year they were saying you were dead."

Out in the hall, Adrienne was telling Garrison to *hide* that *box* in the *trunk* because it was a *surprise*. The hall door clicked open and clicked shut again. I took my mug and sat down.

"Anyway," I said, "I got a couple of the details wrong, but Barbara doesn't seem to be noticing. She thinks I'm a genius. Or maybe a witch. But they found out where he got the needle—actually, a plunger and a supply of needles. He just walked into a doctor on some Godforsaken side street in St. Louis and asked for a prescription for wasp-sting antidote. Makes me think Darcy Penter should give up politics and go back to biology."

"Everybody should give up politics and go back to biology," Phoebe said. "Or give up politics and not do anything. I'd be willing to support the entire United States House of Representatives for life if they just promised to go home and not do anything ever again."

"Especially to the tax code," Nick said.

"I didn't think about the politics thing until we were practically home," I said. "Maybe that's because thinking about how Evelyn took us in makes me feel like an ass, and the more obvious it was, the more of an ass I feel. I mean, nobody on earth collects money for right-to-life *and* right-to-choose."

"I figured that out," Phoebe said. "It was something Tempesta said. That she never trusted Evelyn because all the conservative groups Evelyn was involved in were ones she hadn't heard of. She said the conservative charitable community is actually fairly small. Everybody knows everybody. But she never knew Evelyn except as a publicist."

"What's Tempesta doing these days?" I said.

"Trying to convince her husband to send his bodyguard to a—I don't remember what they're called. For mentally retarded adults, where they live in a house with a lot of other mentally retarded adults and a normal-intelligence caretaker."

"A community house," I said. "What are you talking about?"

"That was the business with all the vandalism she kept taking the rap for and didn't do," Nick said. "It was driving me crazy. So I got her alone and found out. Her husband has this bodyguard who's sweet enough most of the time, but he's not bright and he can't really think things through. So he hears the Downtown Church is a bad, evil place and he gets all worked up and goes hauling off to do something about it. The same with the abortion clinic. Tempesta likes the man. She didn't think it was fair for him to get into serious trouble when all he was doing was trying to do the right thing. So—"

"I think I'm going to have a headache," I said.

"The chalk," Nick said.

"Right. Well, you were right and I was wrong. That was put on the money in New York, at the Toliver-Campion Trust. Actually, it was done years ago, when Jon first converted his money to cash. You were the one who told me how crazy his trust officers got about it. One of them was this really old man who'd been with the Trust since the Depression. He remembered the chalk from the days they'd tried to use it for kidnappers. When Jon put all that money in his safety-deposit boxes, this man just had it all dusted. It had been lying around waiting to go blue for ages. Barbara said it was a good thing Jon turned out to be crazy after all."

"Well, the bank could have had a little trouble with lawsuits if he hadn't," Nick said.

"If it had been on the money all that time," Phoebe said, "why didn't Jon know about it?"

"He did. He just never thought it was anything but a nuisance and an insult. He really took incredible chances. You know the prescription dope he drugged Margaret Keeley and Evelyn with?"

"I knew we'd get to that," Nick said.

"There's nothing to get to," I said. "The doctor he got the wasp-poison antidote from had a locked cabinet in his examining room, full of the stuff. Jon just waited for him to go out of the room, busted into the thing—and it wasn't subtle, from what I hear. He just broke this little glass window it had and took a handful at random. They found the rest of the stuff in one of his suitcases. Butazolidin. All kinds of nonsense. And— There's the door again. Adrienne must have locked herself out."

I put my coffee cup down and went into the hall, not particularly worried about the fact that I was dressed in nothing but a calf-length T-shirt sleep thing from Saks and one of Nick's flannel shirts. Garrison had watched me grow up, and everybody else was family.

I stepped over cardboard boxes full of wrapped gifts and suit carriers full of Adrienne's party clothes and an unidentifiable soft package wound with silver wrapping paper with a bow on top. I also stepped over the cat, who was trying to take up residence in an open hatbox. What I was doing with a hatbox, or why it was open, I didn't know.

"I put that key on a ribbon so you'd wear it around your neck," I said as I swung the door open. "I don't want to worry about you— Oh Christ."

"Hello, Pay," David Grossman said.

"What are you doing here?" I said.

"Looking for Phoebe."

I sighed. Like Phoebe, David was short and roundish and cherubic-looking—most of the time. At the moment, he seemed close to suicidal. His plain blue suit was wrinkled. His plain white shirt had a yellow stain on the collar. His tie was something he should have been talked out of buying in the first place. A large part of me wanted to haul off and kick him hard enough to crack his kneecaps. He deserved it. He did not, however, *look* like he deserved it. He looked like he was going to sweat himself into dehydrated death.

"Pay?" he said.

"Look," I said. "I'm going to close this door. Then I'm going to go into the kitchen. If she wants to let you in, I don't suppose it's any of my business."

"It's your apartment, Pay."

"You couldn't prove it by what goes on around here."

I swung the door shut, stared at it for a moment and then marched back into the kitchen. The cat had preceded me. She was sitting in Phoebe's lap, licking drops of cream from Phoebe's extended index finger. Nick was sitting on the far side of the table, reading the *Post* story about me and laughing silently and convulsively. I snatched the paper out of his hands and threw it on the floor.

"You," I said to Phoebe. "The doorbell was for you."

"David?"

"I shut the door in his face. I think he's still standing in the hall, waiting to be let in."

"Oh."

"Don't do it," Nick said. "He's a jerk."

Phoebe got up and left the room. We heard the door open in the hall, and the low murmur of voices, and the sound of footsteps going toward the living room.

Nick said, "Whoosh."

My coffee cup was nearly empty. I refilled the kettle with water and put it back on the stove.

"Does he have anything like an explanation for why he's been behaving the way he's been behaving?" I said.

"I don't know, McKenna. I haven't been talking to him."

"Not at all?"

"I've cursed him out once or twice. I've made some statements on what I consider to be the state of our partnership, meaning over. Pay, I've known Phoebe all my life. We both came up from the same place in the same way, and we kept each other from going crazy in the years we were adjusting to not being poor anymore. Which is a hell of a lot harder to do than you'd think."

"You tell me that once a month," I said. "Usually when my mother comes in to take Adrienne for lunch."

"Your mother runs around in a 1936 Rolls-Royce Silver Ghost with a uniformed driver. It's a good thing she's a nice woman."

"What does this have to do with David?"

"Nothing. But you ought to be glad I'm a pacifist sort. He's out there in the living room and I'm not wringing his neck."

The whistle went off on the kettle. I took the kettle from the stove and poured the water into my not quite automatic coffee machine. It was made of wood and looked pretty, but it was just as much trouble as the old grind-and-drip.

"I wonder how the baby really is," I said.

"We can't know until it's born. Spina bifida is funny. Maybe Benjamin will be born severely damaged and die in a couple of days. Maybe he'll be born only a little damaged and they'll take care of it at the hospital before Phoebe brings him home, and three years from now we'll never be able to tell he had it. I'm with Phoebe. Have him, hope for the best and see what happens."

"Me, too," I said. "I wonder what they're doing out there."

The hall doorway slammed open. Adrienne said, "Could you get the big bear, Garrison, please? In the lumpy package with the bow on top. I think Nick wrapped it himself. And the box with the little presents in it. They're for stockings."

"Of course, Miss Adrienne. What about your dresses?"

"I want to hang them on the hook in the front. And don't look in the box, because one of the little presents is for you. Christmas is such a *problem.* I'm going to give my room one more look."

"I listen to them together and I feel like I'm acting in something on PBS," Nick said. "I hate PBS."

We listened to Adrienne tromping through the hallway toward the back. I bit my lip.

"Oh dear," I said, "you can't get to the back hall except by going through the living room."

The hallway door clicked again: Garrison going out. Adrienne's footsteps stopped. We heard her let out a sigh. We heard her reverse course and head back toward us.

She came through the door from the hallway, marched to the middle of the kitchen and put her hands on her hips.

"Phoebe and David," she said, "are *necking.*"

"Shit," Nick said.

"I'm not allowed to use that word," Adrienne said, "but I feel exactly the same way. How can I supervise the packing? I can't go barging in and out of there to get to my bedroom when they're doing *that.*"

"They probably won't be doing it for long," I said.

Adrienne snorted. "The way they look, they'll still be there when we get back from Christmas." She peered at Nick suspiciously. "You're getting that look on your face," she said. "I don't like it."

"You'll understand when you're older," Nick said.

"What look on his face?" I said.

"I'm getting out of here," Adrienne said. "This sort of thing is *embarrassing.*" She went all the way back to the hallway door and stopped again. "And I'm *never* getting married," she said. "As soon as people start talking about getting married, they get weird."

She pushed through the swinging door and disappeared.

"You want to get weird?" Nick said.

## About the Author

ORANIA PAPAZOGLOU was born in Bethel, Connecticut. After graduating from Vassar, she taught freshman English, tended bar and fell in love with a man who is allergic to cats. She knows entirely too many romance writers. *Rich, Radiant Slaughter* is her fourth novel for the Crime Club.

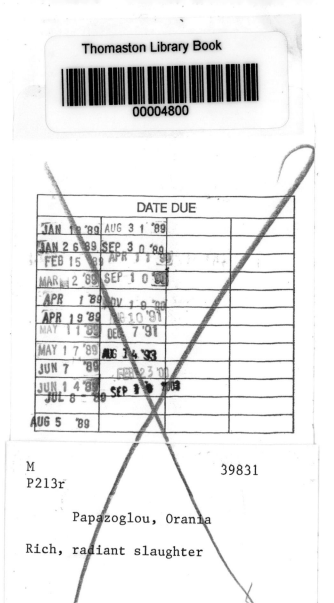